A STONE'S THROW
FROM PARADISE

A Stone's Throw from Paradise

Linda Oatman High

EERDMANS BOOKS FOR YOUNG READERS
GRAND RAPIDS, MICHIGAN / CAMBRIDGE, U.K.

Library of Congress Cataloging-in-Publication Data

High, Linda Oatman.
A stone's throw from Paradise / by Linda Oatman High.
p.   cm.
Summary: Thirteen-year-old Lizzie searches for memories of her
mother while spending a summer with her grandmother
among the Amish in Pearly Gates, Pennsylvania.
ISBN 0-8028-5147-9 (cloth : alk. paper) —
ISBN 0-8028-5142-8 (paper : alk. paper)
[1. Self-acceptance — Fiction.   2. Amish — Fiction.
3. Grandmothers — Fiction.]   I. Title.
PZ7.H543968St   1997
[Fic] — dc20   96-30694
                                CIP
                                AC

For the grandmothers — Nana Emma Millard and Granny Nellie Zook — and in memory of grandparents now angels: Charles Haas, Minnie Haas, and Mark Millard.

With thanks to:

The Society of Children's Book Writers and Illustrators, for serendipity in the form of a work-in-progress grant.

Editors Amy Eerdmans and Karen Klockner, for giving my book wings and helping it to fly.

The Barn Saver John High and our children — J.D., Justin, Kala, and Zach — for being there through sunshine and shadow, and for faith in miracles come true.

CONTENTS

CHAPTER 1

Flying

For as long as I can remember, ever since my real mama got her wings and flew, I've been thinking about flying. Flying and dying, and how it all works. How people leave their worn-out broken bodies behind and whoosh up through the sky, souls whizzing clear to heaven like invisible birds with angel wings.

I love birds — the way they soar magically into the wild blue yonder and never fall down, the way they sing even when a storm is brewing, the way their eyes sparkle like shiny black beads in the sunlight, and the way their feathers are so doggone strong even though they look delicate and weak. I wish *I* could fly.

Pa told me a story once about people of long ago who wanted to make birds even more beautiful than they already are. So these people captured birds and painted their feathers, all fancy swirls and polka dots and stripes of many colors. And guess what happened? The paint made the birds too heavy to fly, and they died falling from the sky. That picture stuck in my mind, just like some of the other images I see when Pa tells stories.

Pa's the best storyteller, and a fine singer, too. Pa sings ballads and lullabies and hymns and 1970s songs he calls golden oldies. He sings a song called "Muskrat Love" that was playing on the radio when he met my mama in the Eat-Your-Heart-Out Cafe in Pearly Gates, Pennsylvania. That song always makes me cry.

Some of Pa's stories make me cry, too, like the one about the last time we saw my mama alive. It was a warm and brilliant morning towards the end of October, the kind of day that makes you think summer will go on forever. The leaves drifting from trees were orange and red and lemon-yellow, and the Pearly Gates sky was a dazzling shade of blue — so radiant it lifted your heart, Pa said. Like the color of Mama's eyes, he added.

"Mama looked so beautiful that morning, Lizzie," Pa would say with a sigh, and I'd know he was still missing her from that deep place nobody else could ever fill. "Her shiny black hair was blowing wispy and soft in the breeze, tickling our faces like tiny feathers as we kissed good-bye."

I always closed my eyes at this part, picturing Mama. "She was wearing a red-and-white Phillies baseball shirt," Pa went on, "faded blue jeans with holes in the knees, and her clunky black work boots." Pa had given me those boots on my thirteenth birthday, and they fit just right.

"I lifted your pudgy little hand and waved good-bye as she got in our shiny red Ford and rolled down the window," Pa said, and this was the part where tears would start trickling across my cheeks. "Mama reached out and squeezed your fingers, blew us some kisses, and then she was gone, fading away into the blue and orange and red and yellow day with her long hair flying in the warm autumn wind."

Pa always paused here, until Mama got smaller and smaller like the disappearing dot at the end of an old movie. I breathed deep, almost smelling the fall air and the perfume I knew Mama always wore called Wind Song. I still had her last half bottle.

"She went to Granny Zook's farm just a mile down the road," Pa continued, his voice raspy and low. Granny Zook was Pa's mother, the Amish grandma I always bragged about in school. Nobody else I knew had an Amish relative.

"Mama fetched the best pumpkin at Granny Zook's for your first jack-o'-lantern," Pa reported proudly. "Huge and smooth and the prettiest orange you'd ever hope to see. Granny Zook said it took Mama almost an hour to choose that pumpkin, roaming up and down the rows in the patch with her eyes squinted toward the ground, choosing exactly the right one for her little girl. She loved you with all her heart, Lizzie Zook."

Pa always stopped there, not telling about Mama's accident on the way home. But still, I couldn't help seeing it: all blood-red and squished orange and broken glass, with the saddest shade of blue framing the crashed-car picture in my mind.

I thought about Pearly Gates a lot, even though I was only nine months old when we moved from Pennsylvania to West Virginia. I thought about

3

Mama's last day in Pearly Gates, and about the little pink house Pa told me we rented back then. I thought about the wide open spaces: the fields and the farms and the sky and the barns. I thought of the fresh Pennsylvania air, and of the horses clip-clopping peacefully upon the roads there, pulling the black and clattering Amish buggies. I thought of how Mama and Pa had both grown up Amish, then left the plain life behind, falling into the world as they fell in love. Pearly Gates is a tiny village where Amish and English — regular people like us — live side by side, and it's a stone's throw from a town called Paradise. My parents both loved it there in Pearly Gates, Pa always said.

I often wondered why they left the Amish, and once I asked Pa.

"We longed for the things of the world," Pa said with a shrug, "things that were forbidden by our parents and by the church, like electricity and cars and television and fancy clothes and rock and roll."

"Was it hard for Granny Zook when you left?" I asked.

Pa sighed. "I reckon it was almost like a death," he said. "I was the baby of the family, and all my brothers and sisters had already left the Amish. I was my mother's last hope."

I always looked up to Granny Zook as some sort of a hero or a saint, standing rock solid in faith even when all her hopes were broken. In my eyes, she was some sort of Dutch angel — gauze prayer covering plopped smack-dab like a lacy halo on top of her silver head, the wings of her long black dress ready to launch

4

her off to the Promised Land. Granny Zook looked as if she could fly.

When I thought of Granny Zook, I 'specially wished I could fly. If I could, I'd fly right over the Shenandoah River and the Blue Ridge Mountains, zooming away from the place we lived now.

Ever since we moved to West Virginia, Pa and I had lived in the Shady Acres Estates Mobile Home Park, where there wasn't even one shade tree, except on the owner's lot, and there sure weren't any estates. Marooned halfway up Hairy Hog Hill on a patch of skunkweed and poison ivy, Shady Acres reminded me of a parking lot for beached submarines: twelve trailers, laid out in rows of three across and four down, with just enough yard for each family to park a couple of Big Wheels and Tonka trucks. We were Lot Number Seven, and all I ever saw through the windows was the glaring aluminum of other trailers and kids arguing over bikes.

Ours was a silver-and-green submarine — ten by fifty feet of aluminum siding, puke-green carpet, and fake-wood walls. The toilet didn't flush right, and there was a little hole where the bathroom floor had rotted through, and you could look straight down to the ground. I always wondered how it would be to have a solid foundation underneath and to live in a house without wheels . . . a home without a hitch. Whenever a big storm came, I was afraid that our trailer would blow right off Hairy Hog Hill, and land up in Oz or somewhere.

"Soon as our ship comes in, we'll buy us one of those double-wides with three bedrooms and a fireplace," Pa always said. "Central air and a patio, too."

Pa would grin, and I just never had the heart to tell him that no ship was ever coming in to Shady Acres Estates, unless it sprouted some hill-climbing wheels.

What *did* blow into Shady Acres and right into our trailer was Mae, my new stepmother. Whirling her way into our lives a year ago and trying to take over everything, she insisted I call her Mae-Mama. Her name sounded like the month of May.

"I want to be your friend *and* your mother, sweetie," she said at the ritzy wedding with a show-off waterfall cake. I despised that cake, and half wished it would just crumble to pieces, like my old life did when my new mother swirled in with her pansy-spangled dresses and shiny rose lipstick.

CHAPTER 2

Fake Flowers

It was late in May, right after the new baby Lucas was born, that I lost my bedroom and ended up in the space I call The Cubbyhole. It's a little off-the-hallway storage space usually used as a laundry room with a washer and a dryer, but ours held me and my single bed, along with my clothes and a gold-framed picture of Mama that watched over me as I slept. Pa and I had always used the Shady Acres laundromat, so The Cubbyhole was being wasted for all these years, according to Mae-Mama.

I was trying to finish my homework as Mae-Mama washed her dusty plastic flowers in the kitchen sink. I hated fake daisies and their synthetic smell, but Mae-Mama acted as if they were picked straight from the Garden of Eden. She had fake flowers on the counter dividing the kitchen from the living room, flowers sprouting from the top of the fridge, flowers on the TV, even blooming red flowers planted on the toilet tank in a big clay pot that belonged to my real mama. My *real* mama used to like *real* flowers.

"Did you happen to watch the Oprah show yesterday?" I called to Mae-Mama, yelling over Lucas's high-pitched wails. Lucas was propped at the far end of the kitchen table in his reclining infant seat, looking like a wiggling sack of flour, his face beet-red and scrunchy above a green terry-cloth sleeper that smelled like pee. All Lucas ever did was poop and pee and eat and cry, poop and pee and eat and cry — a never-ending circle of stink and mess and noise.

"I missed Oprah the last couple of days," Mae-Mama replied, shaking out the flowers and piling them up to dry in the dish drainer. "What was it about yesterday?"

"Decorating your home," I shouted. "I watched it at Jo-Lynn Walker's house." My best friend Jo-Lynn had a home without a hitch, a real mama, a father who didn't work in the coal mines all the time, and a baby brother who knew how to giggle and gurgle and coo.

"And guess what Oprah said?" I asked, as Lucas screwed up his face and let loose with another holler. That kid had a set of lungs the size of China, and his face reminded me of an old elf-man or something.

Mae-Mama zoomed in on Lucas, swooping him out of the seat and unbuttoning her flowered dress in one quick sweep. She perched on the chair next to me at the round table, attaching Lucas to her chest. Our knees touched and I scooted away, metal chair legs screeching across the faded olive-green linoleum. That linoleum was sort of like Mae-Mama: it swirled and whirled and had lots of ugly flowers.

"Oprah said that nobody should ever decorate

8

with plastic flowers," I said, looking at my English paper. I didn't like seeing Lucas's ears move when he nursed. "Oprah said that fake flowers are tacky."

Mae-Mama was quiet for a while, and there was only the buzzing hum of the refrigerator, the ticking of the cat clock's tail, and the disgusting slurpy swallows and sloshing sounds coming from Lucas.

"Oprah has enough money to buy real flowers, hon," Mae-Mama finally said. "We don't."

I didn't look up, just kept staring at lists of prepositions and verbs and nouns. The screen door creaked open and Pa's coal-dusted boots trudged into my corner-of-the-eye line of vision.

"Hey, Mae," he said, and I heard the smack of their kiss. "Hey, Lucas. Hey, Lizzie." Of course I came last, and somehow I knew that I always would from now on.

I concentrated on making perfect sentences, sharp pencil pointing the way for gray words looping across blue lines on white paper. Neat and orderly, like I wished my life would be. And if I just kept writing, I wouldn't have to see what I didn't want to see: my Pa smooching with a lady who wasn't my real mama, the bouquet of purple plastic roses in the center of the table, Mae-Mama's enormous blue-veined breast rising like a white mountain over Lucas's red face. I was mortified that Mae-Mama was so matter-of-fact about nursing her baby wherever she pleased: in the middle of McDonald's, in church, on the front stoop, in the parking lot of Wal-Mart. I just thought that nobody should display their privates in public.

"How was school, Lizzie?" asked Pa.

"Okay," I said with a shrug, folding my homework paper into a tiny square, pushing hard into the creases as Pa took Lucas, holding him up against his shoulder and patting the sweaty green terry-cloth back. Lucas let loose a huge belch, and then there was a squishy liquid explosive noise from the back of his diaper.

"Gross," I said, holding my nose as Pa laid Lucas on a white changing pad on the kitchen floor. We didn't have room for one of those fancy changing tables like Jo-Lynn's family had: blue and pink wicker, with powder and lotion and wipes and cream all lined up in tidy rows of good-smelling stuff.

"This makes me sick," I said. "Turns my stomach." Pa unsnapped Lucas's sleeper and slid out one wriggly leg, then the other. Pulling away the tapes, he lifted Lucas's icky bottom from the yellow goo in the disposable diaper, holding him by the ankles and swiping the stuff with an old washcloth as Mae-Mama whisked out the diaper and swiftly folded it into a smelly lump.

My real mama used real diapers. Pa had told me about how the white cloth looked flapping on the washline behind the little pink house, clipped to the line with yellow duck clothespins. Mama had taken such care to get my diapers perfectly clean and soft, Pa said, first swishing them in a solution of strong bleach and cold water, then hot washing in Ivory Snow. He said that Mama loved how they smelled drying in the sunlight — all pure and fresh and wind-blown.

"Don't be ridiculous, Lizzie," said Mae-Mama, tossing the wadded diaper into the trash can. "The bowel movements of breast-fed babies don't have a bad smell. It's the ones who drink formula that have sour diapers. Bottle babies."

Bottle babies. Like I'd been forced to become at the age of nine months. "You were a breast-fed baby, too, Lizzie," Pa explained, when Lucas was born. "After your mama was gone, you rooted for her milk for months, burrowing into my chest and pulling my shirts and scratching on my neck all frustrated and mad. You refused strained juice and oatmeal and all those jars of baby food people gave us."

Pa was sprinkling powder on Lucas's bottom as Mae-Mama grabbed another diaper from the stack on the counter and positioned it beneath the baby. It made me sad how they did everything so well together, almost as if they were one person with four arms.

"Hope he smells better now," I muttered, as Pa nuzzled the fuzz on Lucas's head and Mae-Mama stuffed his legs back into the sleeper. I stuck my homework paper in the pocket of my backpack, then stood with a yawn and a stretch. Seventh grade was tiring, and so was Lucas's crying. I felt like going to my own little space and taking a nice long nap, maybe from now until Lucas grew up.

"Lizzie, peel six potatoes for supper, please," Mae-Mama said, as Pa cranked the handle on Lucas's baby swing, winding it up while Mae-Mama arranged Lucas in the canvas seat.

Sighing, I opened the cupboard beside the fridge and yanked out a bag of potatoes. It was a wonder Mae-Mama used *real* potatoes, not the instant fake kind.

Towering over the low counter, I dropped half-a-dozen rough-skinned brown potatoes with eyes into the silver sink, reaching into a drawer for the peeler. Mae-Mama had reorganized *everything* when she moved in: the food, the furniture, the knives and spoons, even me and Pa.

Scraping away at the potatoes, I tried not to notice that Mae-Mama and Pa were hugging. Staring at the curls of peel piling up in the sink, I watched brown become green become white. I twisted eyes from the skin, tossing them like pennies into a well, wishing that Mae-Mama and Pa would stop kissing. I wished that Lucas would stop crying. I wished that my mama had never gone for that pumpkin. I wished that I could fly . . . away from this room and this trailer and this life, right into a fairy tale place that had no stepmothers or noisy babies or potato-peeling chores. A happy-ending kind of a place, where nobody ever died or cried or felt sad and alone and scared.

A piece of potato peel was stuck to one of Mae-Mama's fake flowers, and I didn't care. I left it there as I slid Pa's lunchbox and the stack of mail further down the counter with my elbow and piled clean potatoes in a pan.

Then I noticed the top envelope of today's mail: a letter from Granny Zook. It was her squiggly and thin handwriting, sloping up in a crooked address towards the pink rose stamp. The blue envelope was addressed to Mr. Jake and Miss Lizzie Zook . . . not Mae-Mama, not Lucas. Just us.

"Hey, Pa," I said. "What did Granny Zook have

to say?" The letter had been opened; the top was all ragged and torn.

"Lots," said Pa. We hadn't seen Granny Zook in almost two years, but she kept in touch with long letters about once a month. "Her garden's all planted, she's looking for a new horse, her neighbor Elsie had the flu for three weeks, she's hoping we come for a visit this summer, the azaleas are blooming, she needs a summer helper for her roadside stand."

"Why?" I asked, drying my hands and riffling through the rest of the mail. Nothing interesting.

"Well, apparently she's decided to sell quilts at The Zook Nook and still keep up with the produce and baked goods," Pa said. "Hoping for a teenaged helper, she said, on account of not being able to pay a whole lot."

And that's when the seed of an idea was planted, the one that would make my wishes come true. . . . *I* could be Granny Zook's helper, and live in Pearly Gates for the summer. I'd get away from Mae-Mama, and Lucas, and this silver-and-green submarine filled with diapers and stink and noise. I'd go to that miraculous place, Pearly Gates — just a stone's throw from Paradise — where horses clip-clop and real flowers bloom and a little pink house overflows with memories by the side of the road. Fields and farms and blue sky and barns . . . peace and quiet and fresh Pennsylvania air. And maybe if I had a whole summer, not just the usual two-day visit, I'd find out more about my mama.

I'd fly away and search for those things that I just couldn't find here, looking for my real mama where I had lost her — in Pearly Gates, Pennsylvania.

13

CHAPTER 3

The Dawn of a New Day

On the dawn of a new June day, three weeks later, Pa and I were heading for Pearly Gates with my suitcases stacked beneath the seat of Pa's old truck. I can talk Pa into anything, if I set my mind to it.

At first, he was dead set against the idea. Pa and I had never been apart, not even for more than a day. But after I made him see all the perks of my plan (stuff like learning job responsibility and earning some money for next year's school clothes, along with grow-ing closer to Granny Zook and having some indepen-dence for the first time in my life), he finally gave the okay. My next step was writing to Granny Zook. And then I was in business: a soon-to-be summer employee of The Zook Nook in Pearly Gates, Pennsylvania.

"Are you sure you can handle a *whole summer* with Granny Zook?" Pa fretted now, having second thoughts as he crossed state lines. "No TV, no hair-dryer, no air conditioning, no electric light, no radio, no movie theater, no video games, no CDs, no me?"

Pa rattled off all the things I wouldn't have. Then I hit him with the main thing I *would* have.

"It'll be a chance to find Mama where I lost her, in the place where I last saw her," I blurted, as we passed picture-postcard scenery, a collage of fields and farms and flowers and barns. Pa's ancient multi-colored pickup seemed to be driving directly into a magnificent red sun that was rising like a place of hope in the Pennsylvania sky ahead. We'd left home in drizzly darkness and traveled a long time before coming into the light.

Pa was quiet for a while, his profile etched against the morning light shining through the cracked truck window beside him. "Lizzie," he finally said, "I've told you everything that I know and remember about your mama."

"I know, Pa," I said, twiddling with a fringe of denim edging the bottom of my cut-off shorts. "You've *told* me everything, but I haven't *seen* it, except in my mind. I've never been inside the Eat-Your-Heart-Out Cafe, where you two met. I've never seen where Mama's parents live . . . where she grew up. I've never seen the tiny hilltop chapel where you got married. I've never seen the little pink house we rented, or the bedroom where I was born. I've never even seen Mama's grave, or the place where her accident happened."

Pa bit his lip, grasping the steering wheel so tight his knuckles were white. "Reckon we were so rushed every time we've been to Pearly Gates, with having only the weekend to visit Granny Zook," he said.

"There just never seemed to be enough time to stop off at the Cafe, or the chapel, or the midwife. I always had to hurry back home, on account of work."

"But what about the little pink house?" I asked. "That's only a mile down the road from Granny Zook's, but we always take the other way into Pearly Gates."

Pa sighed. "So many painful memories there, Lizzie," he said. "It would bring back a lot of hurt, just seeing the place. And the same with the grave, and the place of the accident. I've just never been able to bring myself to take you there, even though I knew it was what you wanted."

"And what about Mama's parents, and her old homeplace?" I asked, even though I knew the answer.

"They wouldn't accept us, Lizzie," Pa said, as always, resignation weighing down his face. "Mama was shunned by her family, because of leaving the Amish. As far as her folks were concerned, Mama died long before she really did."

"And they don't even *know* us," I said, slumping down in the seat. Pa might sit still for this shunning stuff, but I didn't. And I wouldn't. I was going to find Mama's parents, sometime this summer, and visit them. Mama was a part of them, and I was a part of Mama, and they were going to have to accept me whether they liked it or not. They might have turned their backs on their own daughter, but they were going to have to look Lizzie Zook right in the eye.

We rumbled along in silence, the duct-tape-patched seat scratching my legs. Pa's truck had torn up about fifty pairs of Mae-Mama's nylon stockings in the past year, every Sunday on the way to church. We belonged to the Grace Fellowship Tabernacle, where folks didn't care if your stockings were torn or not. In fact, nobody paid any mind to how anybody dressed, because we believed that what mattered was a person's heart. The *inside* was important, not the *outside*, and if God didn't fuss about gussying up for church and dressing to impress on Sunday mornings, why should we?

I knew I'd have a lot to get used to in Granny Zook's church, where there were so many rules it made my head spin: no shorts, no T-shirts, no bare skin except for the hands and face, no red or orange, no denim, no high heels or sneakers or sandals, long black dresses for married ladies, purple for single girls, straight pins and snaps instead of buttons, beards for married men, bowl haircuts for single boys, black pants for all males, black stockings for all females, black clodhopper shoes for everybody. I wondered if I would have to dress Amish when church time rolled around. The thought made me snicker, and Pa looked at me.

"What's so funny?" he asked, as we passed a pen of fat pink pigs groveling in mud, then a meadow dotted with hundreds of black-splotched white cows. We were getting close to Pearly Gates.

"I was just thinking that maybe I'd dress in Amish clothes for church at Granny Zook's," I said, looking down at my shorts and T-shirt, sneakers and orange glow-in-the-dark pumpkin socks. I collected anything with pumpkins, ever since I was old enough to understand how Mama died.

Pa laughed. "I couldn't imagine you as an Amish girl," he said. "Although you would probably look a lot like Mama did when she was young."

I hushed up for a while, letting that thought sink into my soul. I'd look a lot like Mama — I couldn't think of anything better.

Pa swung around a yellow-beaked chicken pecking in the middle of the road, and I rolled down my window, breathing deep of the fresh Pennsylvania air. It smelled like berries and sunshine and lilacs and newly mowed grass.

"The sunshine and the sky always seem brighter here," I commented as we approached the back of an Amish buggy: iron wheels clattering on gray road, a swaying black carriage rolling slowly beneath endless blue sky. Wide open spaces seemed to go on forever, and the air was quiet and peaceful, serene as could be.

Pa puttered alongside the buggy and then the horse, which was pure white and so huge that it actually made my eyes water to behold such an awesome sight. The dazzling white horse cantered fast and smooth as we passed, eyes sparkling dark brown and glossy mane flying free in the summer breeze. It was the most beautiful horse I'd ever seen.

I stuck my head out the truck window and watched the horse until it disappeared, listening to the clop of horseshoes on macadam, smelling freshly turned earth and the good aroma of somebody's sausage-and-egg breakfast.

"Lizzie," Pa said, "we're here."

I turned and saw up ahead a meadow without end — acres and acres of green grass shiny with dew. The meadow was brilliant with flowers of many colors. They were wildflowers: clusters of daisies and violets, yellow cuckoo-buds, and lady-smocks of silver-white. And then there was the old familiar sign, rising high and bold and shimmery gold by the side of the road:

WELCOME TO PEARLY GATES —
A STONE'S THROW FROM PARADISE.

"We're here," I breathed, full of wonder. "A stone's throw from Paradise."

And then Pa turned left instead of right, heading a different direction than usual.

"Pa," I said, watching a flock of blackbirds fly like cinders into the sky, leaving this earth behind, "you're going the wrong way."

Pa grinned, driving fast past fields and farms and barns, and pointing through the windshield to a sparkling silver-and-red restaurant perched on a hill. "This is the right way," he said. "We're going to have breakfast at the Eat-Your-Heart-Out Cafe."

With heart lifting and hair blowing in the wind, I leaned through the open window and looked ahead and up, seeing blue sky and sunshine and birds flying high. Suddenly I had the strangest feeling, like maybe Pa's old truck had sprouted wings, and we were taking flight into the most wonderful adventure of my life. It was the dawn of a new day, and we were heading for breakfast at the Eat-Your-Heart-Out Cafe.

CHAPTER 4

Miracles and Scrapple

The Eat-Your-Heart-Out Cafe shimmered in silver and red: sparkling tables of polished aluminum, ketchup-red vinyl booths, glossy silver ceiling, slick red floor, a cherry-colored U-shaped counter lined with maroon stools on spindly silver legs. The waitresses were all decked out in sleek red uniforms with fake silver hearts sewn on over their real hearts and fancy scrolled nametags on the other side.

This was definitely the shiniest diner I'd ever seen, and I tried to imagine Mama and Pa in the days before me, on that snowy winter's day when they ended up sitting side by side at the counter, sipping hot cocoa and getting to know one another. If it weren't for this place — it hit me as I gawked at the restaurant — I might not even exist. Elizabeth Rachel Zook might never have been. It was a weird thought, the idea of no me. I might have been somebody else's kid, but then who would I have been?

A glittery jukebox shone silver chrome and neon

light in the far corner, behind an empty booth. I love jukeboxes; they remind me of that old TV show, *Happy Days*, that Pa and I usually like to watch together.

"Pa," I said, taking his arm, "let's sit back there in the corner booth. There wasn't a jukebox when you met Mama, was there?"

Pa didn't say a word, just stood rooted to the spot with a stupefied expression on his face.

"Listen," he whispered.

"What?" I said, and Pa took a step, cocking his head and squinching his eyes.

"What?" I said again, kind of annoyed. I get cranky when I'm hungry, and I was starving. Pa calls my stomach a bottomless pit, because I like to eat so much.

"'Muskrat Love,'" Pa said, as a tune tinkled into the room, the melody jingling faintly below the busy jangle of silverware and glasses and plates, coins and keys and voices.

Pa began to sing, changing the names and some of the words, a soft serenade of the song he and Mama made into their very own: *"Muskrat Rachel, Muskrat Jake, Do the jitterbug down on Muskrat Lake . . ."*

"Pa," I said, fighting tears as goosebumps danced with the hair on my arms, "it's a miracle. I feel like Mama is *right here* this very minute."

Pa halted his singing and the whole world seemed to stop — then revolve spinning around me and my Pa, standing in amazed wonder on the slick floor of a silver-and-red cafe in Pearly Gates, Pennsylvania.

"I truly believe that Mama is giving us some kind

21

of a sign," I said. "Like it's a good thing for me to come here for the summer. Like I'm finally going to find what I've been looking for all my life."

Pa was dumbfounded, and he just gaped at me as the song came to an end and we moved on, breaking the spell of wonder woven by that old song coming from out of the blue.

"I mean, what are the chances of 'Muskrat Love' playing the minute we walk in, Pa?" I jabbered as we slid into the booth. "A zillion to one, I'd bet. And I didn't even see anybody at the jukebox. Did you?"

Pa was still boggled. I could tell by the way all the color was drained from his face.

"Do you think it's a miracle, Pa?" I asked, as a bubbly waitress named Sadie slid two heart-shaped red menus onto the table. "A sign from above?"

Pa took a big breath, plucking at the menu with jittery fingers. His wedding ring flashed gold in all the silver light reflecting from above, and his finger-nails were rimmed, as usual, with black. "Probably just a happy accident, Lizzie," he said, twisting his ring as he studied the menu. "An unusual coinci-dence. A fluke." Pa was shook up; he couldn't stop fiddling with that darn ring. I watched the engraved initials go around and around: MEZ . . . JAZ . . . MEZ . . . JAZ. Mae Ella Zook, Jacob Aaron Zook. Pa and Mae-Mama were going in circles, and so was my mind.

"Maybe the song was like a blessing from Mama, or a kind of a gift," I insisted. "What's that word that means finding something wonderful when you least expect it — serendipity? That's it! Serendipity in the Eat-Your-Heart-Out Cafe." I liked the sound of that.

Sadie bounced back, all perky and bright-eyed and polite as she waited patiently for our order, red pen poised over a heart-shaped pad. I liked this place, although they did go a bit overboard with the silver-and-red heart stuff.

"Two Farmer's Breakfasts," Pa finally said. "The works."

"Scrapple or sausage or ham?" Sadie asked, and Pa grinned.

"Scrapple, of course," he replied, and in a blink of her blue eyes, Sadie was gone, bouncing away to the kitchen behind silver swinging doors.

"I bet she wears those contact lenses that make your eyes any color you want," I commented, for lack of anything better to say. After "Muskrat Love," normal conversation seemed kind of lame. "Her eyes look fake . . . they're just too blue."

We were quiet and suddenly kind of shy, Pa and I. It had been so long since we were out to eat together, just the two of us. I gazed around at the other customers — Amish and English, skinny and average and fat, white and brown and black, young and old and in-between. All kinds of different people in the Eat-Your-Heart-Out Cafe. I played my own little game as we waited for our food, trying to find two people who might fall in love today.

And then, just as I decided on pairing up a skinny unbearded Amish man with a pale girl in purple, another miracle struck from out of the blue: I smelled

Mama's perfume — a strong whiff of Wind Song — wafting mysteriously through the room on angel wings or something.

I looked at Pa, and he looked away, as Sadie swished up to our table, two steaming Farmer's Breakfasts on a big red tray.

"It was the waitress," Pa said after she left. "She was wearing perfume."

"It was *Mama's* perfume," I said, studying heaps of scrambled eggs and stacks of toast and pancakes and meat. "I'd know that perfume anywhere. Anyway, why didn't we smell it before, if it was on the waitress?"

Pa didn't answer, just closed his eyes to say grace, then dug into his food without looking at me.

We ate in silence, each lost in our own thoughts. I couldn't stop thinking of "Muskrat Love" and Wind Song — two miracles on the same day. A double-whammy of serendipity.

And then Pa topped it off with an amazing proclamation. "I reckon we could swing by the little pink house on our way to Granny Zook's," he said.

I was bowled over, and made Pa repeat himself, just for the sake of hearing the words I'd wished for all of my life. I'd always been too chicken to mention seeing the house, until today. Maybe it was something about being on a long journey together that made me tell Pa what I had been longing for all this time: seeing the stuff of his stories.

"Listen to this, Pa," I said, spooning the mushy brown meat onto my toast. The stuff was squishy, kind of like oatmeal mixed with Spam, but it sure was good.

"This is a quote we learned in English class, and it just popped into my mind: 'An event which creates faith; that is the purpose of miracles.' George Bernard Shaw."

Pa smiled, polishing off a hunk of meat big enough to feed an army. "'Food which satisfies appetite; that is the purpose of scrapple,'" he said. "Jake Zook."

I took another bite, mixing scrapple and pancake and syrup and egg. "What exactly *is* scrapple, anyway?" I asked, and Pa cleared his throat.

"Pennsylvania Dutch delicacy," he said, not meeting my eyes. "Amish sausage. The gourmet grub of Pearly Gates."

"But what's *in* it?" I asked, and Pa scratched his head, leaving two spiky tufts of gray pointing the way to heaven. I'm glad I have Mama's kind of hair: smooth and straight with no cowlicks.

"I was afraid you were going to ask that question," he said. "It's pig's liver pudding, with cornmeal and flour, molded and fried crispy-brown."

"*Pig's liver pudding!*" I demanded, dropping my fork. I've never liked anything with the word *liver* in it. "And what's in *that!*"

Pa looked up at the silver ceiling, squinting. "Oh, pig's livers, of course. And ground-up scraps from pig-butchering."

I swallowed. "Scraps," I repeated, and Pa nodded.

"What kind of scraps?" I asked, half-afraid to hear Pa's answer. That's the thing about Pa: he always tells you straight when you ask him a question, so you'd better be doggone sure you want to hear before you ask.

"Stuff like guts and hooves and snouts and ears," he rattled off, casual as all-get-out, as if maybe what he said wouldn't sink in if he whipped it out fast enough.

I pushed my plate away. "Guts and hooves and snouts and ears," I intoned. "That's disgusting."

Pa nodded, shoveling in another forkful of the stuff, nonetheless. "The Amish don't waste, Lizzie," he said. "You'll see."

I crossed my arms, sinking down in the seat. I didn't want to see *anything* that involved ground-up guts and hooves and snouts and ears. I would never eat scrapple again, not if it was the last food in Pearly Gates. Not if it was the only food on earth, and I was starving to death.

All of a sudden I was tired, and just a little bit scared for the first time about this brave idea of mine. I stared through the window as Pa finished both Farmer's Breakfasts, thinking of all the things that had happened in this magical place of silver and red. We'd had miracles and we'd had scrapple, and I decided I'd take the miracles with me and carry them in my soul like a special secret stone in a pocket. Pa could keep the scrapple.

CHAPTER 5

The Little Pink House

I couldn't wait to see the little pink house where I had come into this world — the place where I had learned to crawl and to pull myself up and to wave good-bye; the place where I had cut my first tooth and cracked my first smile; the place where we had all lived together, Mama and Pa and me.

As we pulled away from the Cafe and coasted downhill, I closed my eyes and brought into my mind the pictures of Pa's stories: a tiny five-room bungalow, painted coral pink with white shutters. The roof was black slate, and Pa liked to tell of a time just after I was born, when the snow was so heavy that it made the roof sag in the middle. But the little pink house stood strong.

"I wonder who lives there now," I said out loud, imagining what it would be like if Pa and I had never moved to West Virginia, if we had stayed on in Pearly Gates, just the two of us . . . together forever. Then I conjured up the most wonderful daydream of how it would be if Mama were there, too — all three of us in the cream-colored kitchen, baking Dutch apple pies in the old coal stove Pa told me about. I opened my eyes and the bubble burst, my pie in the sky fell flat. Mama was gone; Pa and I had left the little pink house for a silver-and-green submarine in Shady Acres.

"I bet it's a young couple with a baby living there now," I said to Pa. "I hope it's still pink."

The house was bordered by Paradise Road in front, railroad tracks in the back, and cornfields on either side. Mama would push me in a stroller up and down the road, Pa said, sometimes running because it made me laugh. As soon as I caught sight of the little pink house with the Victorian gingerbread porch with all the fancy cut-outs of wood, I'd point and squeal one word: *home.* Pa said I always loved to come home.

And now I felt as if I were coming home once more. Coming home to the place where I belonged, but missing one of the people who belonged to me.

We didn't have a good camera when I was a baby, just a cheap automatic that took fuzzy pictures. I have exactly ninety-eight-and-a-half photographs taken inside the house (the half-picture was taken by Pa, and he had accidentally cut off my head) and only one blurry picture taken outside, on a snowy Easter morning. I loved that picture — the little pink house in the background, all cozy and warm and bright, with our family bundled in Sunday best beside the porch. Mama was holding me in her arms, and Pa was looking into my face like I was the best thing this side of the stars. We were going to Easter Sunrise Service, Pa said, and

28

you can tell that it was early because there were streaks of sunrise — purple and orange and pink — in the horizon behind the house where the Pearly Gates earth meets the sky. Pa said that my first Easter turned out to be one of those rare days when you have sunshine with snow. Mama buried colored eggs in the snow, and Pa searched for them with me in a baby sling on his back.

And now Pa was searching for the little pink house, with me sitting by his side, almost as tall as he was. Funny how time changes some things so much, yet other things stay the same. Like love, and Easter, and little pink houses with white shutters. I just knew, from somewhere deep and sure inside of me, that our house would be exactly the same, even though Pa and I had changed.

I bent down and yanked my blue suitcase from beneath the truck seat, unzipping the pocket and fishing out my camera. I'd take a fine outside picture of the little pink house on a sunny June day, and keep it forever by my bed, along with the photograph of Mama. I wondered if the tulips Mama planted were blooming yet.

"We're almost there, Lizzie," said Pa. "It's just around this corner."

I sat up straight, camera on my lap, heart pounding so hard I could hear it in my ears. I could hardly wait.

"It'll be on my side," Pa said, slowing down as we started to round the curve. I put my finger on the snap of my camera, getting ready, hoping I wouldn't cry and mess up the picture. I took a deep breath, feeling a rumble of pancake and egg and toast and scrapple far down in my stomach.

"Maybe the new people will let us go inside," I said. "Look around for old time's sake, and maybe we'll find one of my baby toys behind a radiator or something. And you know how I felt like Mama was with us, in the Eat-Your-Heart-Out Cafe? Well, can you even imagine how it will feel in the *house?*"

Pa began to sing, trying to be silly, even though I knew he was nervous and scared. *"I've been lookin' for the pink house,"* he sang, to the tune of "I've Been Workin' on the Railroad," *"All the live-long day. I've been lookin' for the pink house, where I lived with Rachel and my baby. . . ."*

I held my breath as we went around the turn, fixing my eyes to the left side of the road and seeing blue sky and sunshine and cornfields green and high. Pa's song came to a shocked halt, as the truck squealed to a stop on Paradise Road. The little pink house was gone.

CHAPTER 6

Broken Hopes

I stared at downy white clouds, feeling as though our house had up and flown away like Mama — just whooshed through the sky, whizzing straight to heaven and leaving us behind to cry.

Tears plopped from my cheeks onto the camera as Pa steered the truck off the road and into the rutted field where the house had been. Pa's face was dragged down with sorrow, and I was downright heartsick, sitting there looking at the empty spot that once held a home.

"I'm sorry, honey," Pa said, voice breaking as he switched off the ignition. The truck coughed and died, and we sat in tongue-tied silence, with only the chirps of singing birds, the cornfields, a couple of trees, the sky, and an airplane flying way up high. "I should have brought you here long before now, Lizzie, no matter how seeing the house would have made *me* feel. I'm so sorry."

"That's okay," I mumbled, leaning down to shove

the camera away, wishing that Pa hadn't seen my tears. "It was just an old house, anyway." I sat up straight, gazing at wispy trails left by the airplane, white paths that led to nowhere. I wondered if all those people on that plane thought they were taking flight into the greatest adventure of their lives, like I did an hour ago. Nobody should ever think like that, because all they'll end up with is broken hopes and dreams. I blinked, squishing away the stubborn image of a tiny pink house with white shutters and a black slate roof.

"It was our home, Lizzie," Pa said, his skinny body sagged into the truck seat. "And that's what made it so important." I nodded, not knowing what to say. Words couldn't make anything better, anyway.

"I wonder why it was knocked down," Pa said, taking off his mirrored sunglasses. His eyes were criss-crossed with fine red lines, like the wrinkled old road maps in the truck's glove compartment.

I shrugged, biting my lip, and Pa swung open his door. "There *is* one thing you can see," he said, trying to smile. "Come with me."

I took a deep breath, pushed open my door, and stepped out. My sneakers sunk into newly plowed dark earth, and some clumps of dirt crumbled through the frayed tops of my pumpkin socks. I followed Pa, shaking from the long day. It was late morning, still early, yet it felt like an eternity since we'd left Shady Acres.

"It's right over here," Pa called, striding towards a tall old fat-trunked tree with waxy leaves of summer green. This was probably the same tree that was dropping all the orange and red and yellow leaves on the

32

autumn day when Mama went to get the pumpkin at Granny Zook's.

Pa walked up to the tree and peered at the bark, then turned and motioned to me. "Come see," he said.

I traipsed to the edge of the field, where the old tree sprawled high and knotted above the earth, its gnarly branches seeming to hug the sun. Pa pointed, zeroing in on the faint worn shape of a carved heart, wrapped around the initials JAZ + RAZ + ERZ. Jacob Aaron Zook plus Rachel Anna Zook plus Elizabeth Rachel Zook. Three people who equaled one family, all those years ago.

I traced the letters, then the heart, and then I clinched the tree. Just put my arms around that rough old scratchy trunk and hugged for all I was worth, embracing the tree and everything good that it stood for. And then I dropped my arms and let go, releasing the tree, along with all the hopes I'd had for seeing the little pink house. I'd had enough miracles for one day, anyway, what with all the unexpected serendipity that came my way in the Eat-Your-Heart-Out Cafe. After all, a person couldn't ask for anything more than three miracles in one day, could they? This wasn't so bad: the little pink house was gone. Houses, like people, can fly away at any time, I guess. Nothing lasts forever.

Pa put a hand on my shoulder and we hiked back to the truck, which was leaning crooked at the edge of the field. The clip-clop of hooves was coming closer and closer as we walked, and finally a horse galloped into sight, gracefully rounding the curve, gleaming white in the morning light. With a start, I saw that it was the same horse we'd passed on the way into Pearly Gates. It was an enormous, pure white horse . . . the most beautiful horse I'd ever seen.

The reins were held by an Amish boy, maybe about my age, and he drew to a fast stop, stones scattering as the horse reared back its head and stomped huge hooves, snorting. There was something strange dangling from the roof of the buggy: a cluster of bright blue feathers, beaded and hung on a strand of leather — like the feathers you win at county fairs — swaying alongside a faded pair of those old fuzzy dice people used to hang in cars. Music was booming from within the carriage, almost rocking the buggy with drumbeats so loud and low they pounded into my broken-hope soul.

"Pa," I whispered, my hand on the handle of the truck door, "I thought that Amish weren't allowed to have radios. And look at those feathers and dice. I never saw anything like that on a buggy before."

"Oh, some of the teenagers rebel and get rowdy, before they officially join the church of the Old Order Amish," Pa replied, as the boy swung down from the buggy, guiding the horse to the side of the road. "The old folks call it 'sowing the wild oats.' They figure that if the kids don't go wild when they're young, they might end up leaving the Amish, so the parents just kind of look the other way when the teenagers hide radios in the buggies and such. They don't like what their kids are doing, and they surely don't approve of it, but they just pretend they don't see. It's as if they're wearing blinders, like that horse, seeing only straight ahead into the future when their children decide to settle down and join the church."

"Did Granny Zook let you sow your wild oats?" I asked, as the boy sauntered our way.

Pa nodded. "But I had my mind made up long before teenaged days," he said. "I was planning to leave the Amish when I turned twenty. Some of us just weren't satisfied with the plain life."

I looked at the boy, who was actually kind of cute, with glossy blonde hair and eyes that sparkled like lime Kool Aid on this hot summer's day. His shirt was the same shade of green, set off by black suspenders and the baggy black broadcloth pants worn by all Amish guys. Pa called them barn door britches; they had buttons instead of zippers.

"Hi," he said, tipping his black hat and flashing Pa and me a sociable smile, then reaching into the buggy and turning off the music.

"Howdy," Pa replied, reaching out to pat the horse.

"West Virginia, huh?" said the boy, nodding towards the license plate of Pa's truck. "I guess you're tourists?"

Pa shook his head, smiling. "Nope," he said. "Pearly Gates was once my home. I'm ex-Amish: Jake Zook."

The boy's face lit up. "Lydia Zook, about a mile down the road?"

Pa nodded. "That's my mother," he said. "My daughter, Lizzie here, is spending the summer with her working at The Zook Nook."

The boy glanced at me, and those green eyes were startling to see, like lights shining from beneath the wide brim of black hat. "I know Mrs. Lydia," he said. "She hires me sometimes, to work the crops when it's really hot. She can't take the heat so good anymore, you know."

"I know," I said. "She's pretty old." We looked at each other for a minute, grinning, like some private joke had passed between us.

The boy toed the dirt, suddenly kind of shy. "My name's Daniel Smucker," he said, looking up at Pa. "My family owns this land."

Pa's eyes widened. "Your father is Jonas Smucker?" he asked, and the boy nodded, looking surprised at Pa knowing that.

"We used to rent a little pink house from him, about thirteen years ago," Pa said. "I recollect you being a toddler when Lizzie and I moved away; you were just a few months older than her. Why, every time I carried Lizzie over to pay the rent, you two hit it off like old buddies — just a-giggling away and playing like there was no tomorrow."

I could feel myself blushing, and Daniel Smucker ducked his head, obviously embarrassed, not looking at me. "The pink house sat right over there." He pointed and Pa nodded.

"That was just taken down a couple of months ago, on account of the house being so old that it didn't pass building codes," the boy said. "It was falling apart and no longer safe — 'a fire hazard,' my Pop said — so a fellow called The Barn Saver took it down."

36

"The Barn Saver?" asked Pa, and the boy nodded.

"He's a man who dismantles old barns and houses and chicken coops and tobacco sheds, just takes 'em apart piece by piece and sells all the used building materials. It's a way of making sure the old places live on for another hundred years in a hundred different ways, instead of being knocked over by a wrecking ball and buried in some landfill. Recycling, that's what The Barn Saver calls it."

Pa was having a major brainstorm. I could tell by the fired-up look on his face.

"Is there anything left — of the pink house?" he asked, jamming his hands in the pockets of his jeans and jingling some change.

The boy rolled up his eyes, thinking, as the white horse rested that majestic head on his shoulder. "Well, last I heard, there was the fireplace mantel, a couple of doors, the lightning rods, and the old front porch."

Pa rocked heel to toe, workboots sinking down into the ground as my hopes rose sky high. "The gingerbread porch?" I asked. "With all the fancy wood cut-outs?"

The boy nodded. "It's stored in the man's warehouse, just down the road," he said. "Between here and Lydia Zook's, far down a lane in the woods. There's a bright orange sign at the end, with The Barn Saver and a telephone number written on it."

I looked at Pa and he looked at me. "Miss Lizzie," Pa said, "we'd best hit the road."

I reached over Daniel Smucker's shoulder, patting the white horse's velvety soft nose. The horse nuzzled my hand, his gentle brown eyes a beacon of welcome to Pearly Gates.

"What's his name?" I asked, as the horse bared his big teeth.

"Blizzard," said Daniel. "He was born in a snowstorm, and now this past winter his baby was, too."

"Hi and good-bye, Blizzard," I said. "We need to go. Maybe I'll see you over the summer sometime."

Then, as Daniel Smucker climbed into his buggy and the music began to blare, Pa and I waved good-bye and hustled into the truck. We needed to fly, because miracles don't wait. This might be more serendipity for Pa and me, in the shape of a Victorian gingerbread porch that used to be ours. And maybe, just maybe, it would be ours once more. *An event which creates faith; that is the purpose of miracles.* I was so glad Daniel had come our way — his words had given me back my faith that everything really would be okay. My broken hopes were piecing themselves together, maybe in different shapes than before, but I was on cloud nine once more.

And then, as the beat of Daniel's music seemed to keep time with the drumming inside my heart, Pa started the truck and took off, making tracks on Paradise Road, flying with high hopes in the direction of a gingerbread porch from long ago.

CHAPTER 7

Real Flowers

An hour later, we were pulling into Granny Zook's stone driveway with one gingerbread porch, two blue glass lightning rods, and a log fireplace mantel, all safely stowed in the back of Pa's truck. I was on top of the world, and kept turning around to be sure this had truly happened, that we now really owned parts of the little pink house. This was definitely a day for miracles.

Granny Zook stood behind the painted white counter of The Zook Nook, looking exactly the same as she had two summers ago, when I was eleven and she was eighty-seven. Now I was thirteen, and Granny Zook was eighty-nine, and I just knew we'd get along fine as usual.

Granny Zook never changed — she always looked the same. My grandmother's hair was soft and white as milkweed silk, hanging straight to her waist when she let it down at night. She had light blue eyes like circles of melted candle wax, round and wide behind silver

39

wire-rimmed glasses. Granny Zook was skinny like Pa, so scrawny that her long black dresses hung like sacks on a stick. Her skin was the color of the moon, pale as potato soup, with lots of lines and tiny blue veins creasing her face. When she took off her glasses, Granny Zook had soft purple circles beneath her eyes that put me in mind of a set of wings. That's why I first started thinking that she would fly, back when I was about five — because of those wing-crinkled eyes.

Pa tooted the horn and Granny Zook gave a brisk wave, bustling from inside her roadside stand and out into the sunshine. "Hi, Grossmummy!" I shouted through the truck window, being silly and using the Pennsylvania Dutch word for grandmother that Pa had taught me as soon as I could talk.

"Hello, Miss Lizzie," Granny Zook called. "Hello, Jake."

Pa tooted again, parking the truck beside a tiny gazebo with two swings facing one another. That was Granny Zook's "take a break place," the wooden swing from which she had a bird's eye view of Pearly Gates.

We hopped out, and I looked around: Granny Zook's white stucco farmhouse with dark green shutters and a wrap-around porch to match, the milky white barn with a star-shaped window on top, the picket fence circling the meadow where Granny Zook's only cow grazed with two plump sheep. Just the way I remembered it. This farm used to have hundreds of animals back when Pa was a kid and his father was still alive, but now, with Granny Zook so old and alone, there were only a few.

But there were hundreds of flowers — *real* flowers: lilacs and lily of the valley flowers, violets and candy-tufts and roses of many colors. I took a deep breath, breathing in the fragrance, so glad to be there. I loved real flowers.

Granny Zook was tromping towards us, heavy black shoes skittering through the stones. I often wondered how Amish people could stand summer-time, what with all those clothes. Granny Zook always wore ankle-length, long-sleeved black dresses, thick black stockings, a prayer covering, and heavy black shoes. When she went out in public, she added a long black bonnet and flowing black cape, like all the Amish ladies in Pearly Gates.

Once, when I was about nine, I asked Granny Zook why the Amish dress like that.

"The Bible tells us to be covered," Granny Zook replied. "So, we cover."

And covered she was. But for some reason, Granny Zook never sweated. Pa said he reckoned it was because she was so used to being hot that her body never even noticed it was overloaded with clothes. It was all she ever knew, Pa said.

Granny Zook's face looked cool now, even on this June afternoon. She spread her arms in welcome, the winglike sleeves of her dress loose and flowing.

Pa hugged her first, then I did. Granny Zook was one of the few Amish people Pa knew, he told me, who showed emotions with displays of affection like hugs and kisses. That was one of the reasons he and Mama left the Amish, Pa said, because they wanted to show their love. Neither Mama nor Pa had ever seen a married Amish couple hold hands in public . . . never. It just wasn't done.

But Granny Zook was holding my hand now. "How you've grown, Lizzie Zook," she said, squeezing my fingers between her frail, brown-spotted hands. Granny Zook was full of love; she never would have shunned Mama and Pa when they left the Amish, even though her best hopes were broken.

"She's all ready for a summer of hard work," Pa said with a wink, as Granny Zook led us through the yard, across the porch, and into her kitchen.

Granny Zook's kitchen was much different than ours. It was a huge room that echoed, bigger than three of our rooms put together. There was a wooden farm table lined with benches, a sprawling wood stove for heat, the most enormous sink you'd ever want to see, and a big gas stove with two tiny orange pilot lights of fire showing through holes in the middle. The Amish don't believe in electricity, so everything that needed power was run by gas: Granny Zook's refrigerator, the hot water, the old wringer washing machine, the lights. Nighttime always looked different at Granny Zook's, on account of the gas lights being so dim and hissing and blue-flared. They had a funny smell, too, that kind of tickled my nose and burned my eyes.

"I made a special lunch for you two," Granny Zook announced, trudging across the worn linoleum floor to the refrigerator.

"Chicken pot pie," Pa and I said at the same time, as Granny Zook heaved out a cast-iron kettle. We loved

Granny Zook's chicken pot pie, with her special home-made noodle squares and Silver Queen corn and the good-smelling deep orange seasoning powder called saf-fron. Granny Zook told me that saffron was made from the flower of a crocus — a *real* flower — and that the powder cost lots of money to buy in the store.

Granny Zook clomped to the stove, plopped the kettle on a burner, and spun a dial. A blue-orange flame leaped around the edges of the kettle, and my stomach growled. I couldn't wait to eat.

Pa went to the refrigerator and opened it like he owned the place, lifting out a mason jar. I knew what it was: Granny Zook's homemade non-bubbly root beer, made from real roots and herbs. We always drank that here.

"How have you been?" asked Granny Zook, stir-ring away at the kettle.

"Oh, just wonderful, Mum," said Pa, pouring three cups of root beer.

"And the new wife and boy?" Granny Zook opened a cupboard and took out a loaf of the bread she baked every day.

"Mae and Lucas," Pa said, and the names rolled like honey on his tongue, making me just a little bit jealous. "They're doing great. The baby's growing like crazy, and Mae can't wait to meet you someday soon. Lucas is just a bit young for the long trip, and we're hoping to buy a car with room for four. It would be too crowded in my truck if I brought the whole family."

The whole family. Somehow, I just couldn't think of Mae-Mama and Pa and Lucas and me as one family.

43

It seemed more like *I* was his first family and *they* were his second.

Granny Zook nodded. "I'm anxious to meet them," she said. "Don't wait too long, Jake. I'm not getting any younger, you know."

Pa just smiled. "You're healthy as a horse, though," he said.

"Speaking of horses," I chimed in, "we met this boy Daniel Smucker who said he works for you sometimes. He has the most beautiful horse named Blizzard."

Granny Zook nodded, setting the table with gigantic blue plates and jumbo spoons. Everything seemed big at Granny Zook's except for Granny.

"Daniel works the crops sometimes," she said. "Chops firewood in the winter, too. The boy has stronger arms and a better heart than mine."

"*Nobody* could have a better heart than you, Grossmummy," I said, taking a sip of root beer. "Except maybe Pa."

Pa went to the kettle, which was steaming and smelling so good I could've eaten the whole thing all by myself. Pa lifted it and carried the hot pot pie to the table, his eyes lighting up as he looked down at our lunch.

"I love this stuff," he said. "This is one thing I miss about being a kid. You'll have to give Mae the recipe, Mum."

We all sat down and joined hands for prayer, which Granny Zook rattled off in Dutch, and then we dug in. We ate and ate and ate: chicken pot pie and bread with strawberry jelly and cup after cup of root beer.

"We had breakfast at the Eat-Your-Heart-Out," Pa said. "Lizzie liked the scrapple." He winked at me.

"Oh, we'll have lots of scrapple," Granny Zook said, missing Pa's wink.

We pushed away our plates, Pa holding onto his scrawny little stomach like he was Santa Claus or something. "I'm stuffed," he said, but when Granny Zook pulled a shoofly pie from the cupboard, Pa changed his mind. Pa and I loved Granny Zook's shoofly almost as much as the pot pie.

"Guess what, Mum?" Pa asked, as we polished off the molasses-and-brown-sugar pie. "Lizzie and I went to take a look at the little pink house we used to rent, and it was gone."

Granny Zook nodded, pushing up her glasses. "The Barn Saver took it down, back in early spring," she said.

Pa grinned. "I know," he said. "We bought the porch, two lightning rods, and the fireplace mantel from him. I'm going to rig them all up at home."

I looked at Granny Zook, wondering how she felt about Pa buying lightning rods. The Amish don't believe in using them, because they think it would be like fooling with God. They figure that if God wants to strike your barn with lightning, that's His decision, and you'd better not mess with Him. They also don't believe in insurance, because they say that the Amish community is their insurance company. Pa told me once that if a barn burns down, that family is believed

45

to be bearing the wrath of God for the whole community, and that's why they all chip in for barn raisings.
The Amish are close-knit people.

"Can't you stay for the day, Jake?" Granny Zook
asked, as we all walked out through the shaded yard
and into the sunlight. Pa put on his sunglasses, shaking his head.

"Sorry, Mum," he said, opening the truck door.
"Mae wasn't feeling real well when we left, so I want
to get on home to help her out. And we get up pretty
early for church tomorrow, and then it's back to work."

Granny Zook sighed, giving Pa a long hug. "Safe
home," she said, which meant to have a safe journey.
"How was the trip coming in?"

"Great," Pa said. "We went from rain into sunshine, soon as we hit Pennsylvania."

"From darkness into light," I added. "It was a
long drive."

And now Pa had the same long drive back home,
except without me. "Safe home," I said, hugging him
and fighting tears.

"Here," I said, reaching down and plucking a
daisy from the ground. "Give Mae-Mama a *real* flower
when you get home."

Pa smiled, taking the flower and putting it on the
dash of his truck. "She can use it to find out if I love
her, or love her not," he said, his voice sounding like
a wink. I couldn't see his eyes behind the sunglasses,
which was probably good, because if I saw even one
tear in Pa's eyes, I'd most likely change my mind and
leave Pearly Gates behind.

Pa reached out and drew me into his skinny arms, nuzzling my hair, then he reached beneath the seat and took out my suitcases, placing them side by side in the yard.

"I'll carry them in," I said. "I'm strong."

But I wasn't feeling so strong when Pa climbed in his truck, starting it up and backing away with a wave. I watched him go, sitting down between Granny Zook and my suitcases, and plucking another daisy.

"I'll miss him, I'll miss him not," I whispered, pulling petals from the flower until the last one. "I'll miss him," I finished, as Pa stopped on Paradise Road and blew me a kiss.

"I'll miss you so much, Lizzie," he called, leaning out the window of his truck of many colors beneath the Pearly Gates blue sky, with parts of our little pink house piled on behind. "I love you."

"I love you!" I shouted, feeling sort of scared and empty and alone as Pa pulled slowly away. "I'll call!"

And then I remembered: Granny Zook didn't have a phone.

CHAPTER 8

A Rude Awakening

Before sunrise the next morning, Granny Zook was up and bustling about, rousing me out of a nice deep sleep. I'm not an early riser, and Pa *never* wakes me in the summertime. But Granny Zook was a different story.

"Rise and shine, Miss Lizzie," sang Granny Zook, standing outside the dark bedroom in her long white nightgown. Her hair was down, and for a minute I thought she was an angel or a vision or a divine holy being, what with all that silver and white. I sat up and blinked, then flopped back on the bed when I realized it was only Granny Zook and not some celestial messenger from Heaven.

She headed for the bathroom, and I reached beneath the feather pillow, fishing out the black flashlight I'd borrowed from Pa. Shining the beam of light on the tall grandfather's clock, I saw the glinting of sharp golden hands that told me it was only five-thirty in the morning. Five-thirty! Nobody in their right mind gets up at that time, except for Pa, who has to go work in a coal mine.

"Rise and shine," I muttered, sweeping the light across the walls of the room that used to belong to Pa. The room was painted robin's egg blue, with lots of cracks and chips in the plaster. Pa had told me once that the walls of Granny Zook's house were made of horsehair plaster, which is mud and limestone mixed with lots of coarse hair from horses in order to make it strong. That's just the way they made walls a hundred years ago, when Granny Zook's house was built. Pa pulled a chunk of plaster from a gap in the hallway wall and showed me the hair, which was all different colors from many different horses. It gave me the heebie-jeebies, thinking of all those dead horses from long ago, helping to hold up Granny Zook's house.

The walls of Pa's old room were almost bare, because the Amish don't believe in photographs and stuff like that. The only decorations on the walls were glass plaques with Bible verses, painted in shades of pink and blue and green and purple. I aimed the light at one in front of the bed, which said, "Blessed is every one that feareth the Lord, that walketh in his ways. Psalm 128:1." Around the words were twines of leaves and vines and delicate pink painted flowers. Pa said the plaque has been there since he was a kid.

Sighing, I decided to rise and shine, or else Granny Zook would be pestering me again. I planted the flashlight beneath the pillow, rubbed my eyes, and dragged myself up. It was hot in here already; my

49

T-shirt was sticking to the backs of my knees. I was used to sleeping in air conditioning back home in the silver-and-green submarine, where my clock radio woke me at a decent hour.

"Rise and shine, Miss Lizzie!" It was Granny Zook again, totally dressed this time, her hair twisted into a neat bun capped by a prayer covering. I couldn't imagine how she got all those clothes on so fast.

"It's time to milk Nellie," Granny Zook said. "And fetch the eggs. Then we'll have a breakfast of scrapple and scrambled eggs."

Scrapple. I winced, making a face as Granny Zook marched away, clumping down the narrow twisting staircase. "Do you have any Froot Loops?" I called, but she was gone.

I wriggled into my shorts and padded barefoot to the bathroom. Granny Zook had pulled up the dark green shade, and I gazed out at the moon, thinking how the same moon hung over Pa and Mae-Mama and Lucas at home. They would still be sleeping, since church doesn't start until ten-thirty at Grace Fellowship.

Church. I'd forgotten all about today being Sunday. Time always seemed to pass slower in Pearly Gates, and I was always getting my days mixed up. What was I going to wear to an Old Order Amish Church? I wasn't ready for this, not on my first day. Pa and I usually just stayed at Granny Zook's while she went out to church, which was held in some Amish person's house. We'd never been there when it was Granny Zook's turn to have church.

I made my way through the hall and down the bare wood steps, which creaked and squeaked beneath my feet. The stairway was so narrow that my body almost touched the banister on one side and the wall on the other. It was a wonder some fat person never got stuck. And the twists! The spiral staircase was so coiled that you had to really pay attention, or else you'd take a header and tumble clear to the bottom, like Pa had when he was two years old.

"Granny Zook," I called as I finally touched the floor leading into the kitchen, "do you have any Cocoa Puffs?"

The kitchen clock chimed six times, and Granny Zook was just an outline in the dark. Then a kerosene lantern flared, illuminating Granny's pale face. "I have cocoa," she said. "But no puffs."

I rolled my eyes, not even bothering to explain that Cocoa Puffs were a kind of cereal. Granny Zook had never seen a television commercial in her life, she didn't read magazines, and most of her grocery shopping was done at the Bent and Dent farm store down the road. It wasn't like she was used to food shopping in the IGA, where there were about a thousand different kinds of cereal.

Granny Zook handed me a basket. "Chore time," she said, heading for the door. I followed, and we stepped out into the blackness of the too-new morning, my bare feet slipping on the dew-slicked porch as the quivering flicker of a kerosene lantern lit our path. Granny Zook picked up a silver milk can from beside the porch swing, and we muddled down the steps and

51

across the dark yard. Birds chirped from somewhere above, and I looked up, yawning. It was too soon in the day for *anything* to feel like singing, if you asked me.

"In the sweet by and by," Granny Zook belted out, bursting into screechy song as we headed toward the chicken house. *"We shall meet on that beautiful shore. . . . "* Singing a hymn at six in the morning! Now I could see where Pa got that habit — from his mother.

The chickens were clucking and Granny Zook was still singing, warbling in a kind of shrill and trembly trill, lifting her voice high as the sky. I guess she was making a joyful noise unto the Lord, and maybe He liked it, but the sound was downright ear-splitting to me. It always gives me a headache when people are too cheery before the sun even rises.

"When the trumpets of the Lord shall sound, and time shall be no more. . . ." Now the chickens were joining in, cackling and crowing and clucking and squawking: a cock-a-doodle-doo of barnyard harmony with Granny Zook leading the glee club.

"The Poultry Tabernacle Choir," I muttered, as Granny Zook plunked down her milk can and yanked open the door of the chicken coop. We stepped inside and it smelled terrible — rooster poop and wet feathers and moldy straw and rotten eggs all mixed into one awful whiff of chicken stink. The straw cut bristly sharp beneath my feet, and it was so dusty. I sneezed as Granny Zook hung the lantern from a hook in the rafters.

52

"Rise and shine!" Granny yodeled, pulling a burlap sack from a low beam and scattering chicken feed in troughs. The chickens came scurrying: Silkies and Bantams and Rhode Island Reds, Black Giants and White Rocks and Blue Cochins and Silver Spangled Hamburgs. Granny Zook had nearly every breed of chicken under the moon — some for butchering and eating, some for egg-laying, some for breeding, some just for pretty.

As the chickens pecked at the feed, Granny Zook looked over at me, her face wavering white above black in the glare of the lantern. "Time to collect the eggs, Miss Lizzie," she said.

I took a step, then stopped. "Granny Zook," I said, "there's poop everywhere, and I'm barefoot."

Granny Zook waved a hand. "Not to worry," she said. "Feet are cleanable, just like shoes. A soul dirties them . . . a soul washes them. That's life."

I took a deep breath, stepping warily and slow, tiptoeing as if I were walking on eggs. It made me queasy, thinking of all the mess beneath my feet, the squishing stink below my toes.

Granny Zook took a bottle of pink liquid from the beam, squirting it into the water trough. "Pig Swig Wormer," she said. "Takes care of roundworm in chickens."

Roundworm. I swallowed, taking a wide path past tailfeathers of black and white and blue and red, thinking of the time when I was five and one of Granny Zook's White Giants flocked me right in the face. I could still see it: a storm of flapping white feathers and red-crested head, yellow beak and black eyes and claws of sharp dark brown with scratchy yellow ridges. The mother chicken had flapped up at me as I walked through the yard, pecking my cheek and flailing my face, all in a tizzy because I picked up one of her chicks. I was *still* leery of chickens, and always watched my step and played it safe, especially with the lady birds.

"Check all the nests, Lizzie," Granny Zook said. "I'm going to get fresh water." She lifted a bucket and tromped out, leaving me alone in the dim coop. As the door slammed shut, I wondered if a mother chicken would attack somebody who picked up one of her eggs. After all, it was still her baby, just not born. *Any* mama would protect her kid, even if it's not out in the world yet.

Eyeing the lines of beak-jabbing chickens on either side of the feed trough, I tiptoed to one of the nests and peered in. There were three brown eggs, speckled dark with dirt and gook and who knows what. I gathered them up one by one, holding the ends with my thumb and finger, trying not to mind how warm and mucky they felt. It kind of grossed me out to think of people eating the unhatched babies of stinky old chickens.

"Get away," I whispered to a blue-clawed, black-feathered chicken who was pecking closer and closer to my feet. The chicken just looked at me, clucked, then strutted away, persnickety tailfeathers sashaying.

I made short work of the job, checking nests and whisking out eggs and wishing that Granny Zook would shake a leg and hurry back. I hated being alone with all these chickens, outnumbered by lots of feathers and claws and beaks and beady black eyes. I hated the stench: rooster poop and wet feathers and moldy straw and rotten eggs, blended with the smelly fumes of the kerosene lantern. It was hot in here, and the air was thick with stink. But through the wire-webbed window of the coop, I could see a beautiful sunrise outside: purple and pink sky, an orange ball of blazing fire. "Rise and shine, my eye," I muttered, plucking two crusty white eggs from a nest.

Granny Zook was finally coming; I could hear her screechy singing. *"Amazing grace, how sweet the sound, that saved a wretch like me. I once was lost, but now I'm found; was blind, but now I see. . . . "*

Then, as the door swung open and Granny Zook trudged inside, I saw something that made me blink my eyes: three colored eggs, blue-green Easter eggs, nestled deep in a nest of straw. I caught my breath, full of wonder and surprise. It was magical — Easter eggs in June. I wondered if maybe they'd been hidden there since April, long forgotten by whichever kids Granny Zook had at her house for Easter dinner. But then I remembered — Granny Zook didn't believe in Easter egg hunts. The Amish think that having egg hunts glorifies a make-believe bunny instead of Jesus, the real reason for Easter.

"Granny Zook," I whispered, but she wasn't listening. That's when the image hit me, the picture of Mama hiding eggs in the snow all those years ago, then Pa and I searching through the yard of the little pink house. Maybe this was another miracle; maybe this was a sign from Mama. Three colored Easter eggs — one for me, one for Mama, one for Pa — welcoming me to Pearly Gates. Serendipity in Granny Zook's chicken coop.

"Granny Zook," I said again, lifting out an egg with a shaking hand. "Look."

Granny Zook pushed up her glasses, peering, then nodded. "Araucanas chickens lay those eggs," she said. "All shades of blue and green, prettiest eggs you'd ever want to see."

Heart falling, I dropped the eggs into the basket with the others. It wasn't a miracle after all, just stupid old blue-egg-laying chickens trying to get my hopes up with their fancy fake Easter eggs.

"All finished, Miss Lizzie," Granny Zook pro-nounced, dumping water into the trough. "Now all we have is the milking, then we'll have a good breakfast of fresh eggs, scrapple, and milk."

Fresh eggs, scrapple, and milk. Nothing could have grossed me out more, on this early morning of my first day in Pearly Gates. Clutching the basket of crusted eggs, I stepped fast from the coop and into pure air, swiping my feet back and forth over moist dewy grass.

"Do you have any Froot Loops?" I asked, as Granny Zook picked up the milk can and swished away, the hem of her long black dress sweeping the wet grass. "Pa and I always eat Froot Loops on Sunday mornings."

But Granny Zook didn't hear; she was making tracks for the barn.

"Rise and shine," I muttered, planting the egg basket in the grass and trailing after Granny Zook. I yawned, wishing I could just go back to bed and wake up at the end of the summer. Didn't Granny Zook realize that teenagers need their sleep?

Granny Zook yanked open the barn door and disappeared within, as I closed my eyes for a minute, trying to clear the sleepies from the corners. I'm always bleary-eyed in the morning, and at home I watch TV to help myself wake up. But here, there was no TV, just chickens and a cow and Granny Zook, along with a couple of dumb-faced sheep.

I opened my eyes, bumbling into the barn to a sight even more disgusting than the dirt of the chicken coop. Nellie the cow was pooping, plopping huge piles of gook into the stall. It turned my stomach, and I stumbled backward through the door, feeling sick as a dog and needing fresh air. I gulped, my eyes finally opened to how hard this summer might turn out to be. It was a rude awakening, on the morning of my first day in Pearly Gates.

CHAPTER 9

Serendipity in Granny Zook's Kitchen

"Where's church today?" I asked as Granny Zook dug into a hog's mess of a breakfast: a conglomeration of scrambled eggs, scrapple, and just-wrung-out milk, fresh from the udders with clots of curdled fat floating on top. *Yuck.* I decided to have toast and root beer.

"Church will be held at Jonas Smucker's down the road," Granny Zook announced. The clock chimed seven times, and I thought of how I'd probably *still* be sleeping at home.

"*Daniel* Smucker's home?" I asked, and Granny Zook nodded, plopping globs of homemade ketchup on her scrapple. A beam of sunlight slanted through the kitchen window, reflecting silver glints off Granny Zook's fork as it went back and forth, up and down. Grossmummy sure liked to chow down.

"What will I wear to church?" I asked, plucking at the frayed denim of my shorts. I'd brought six pairs of shorts, seven T-shirts, one pair of jeans, a jacket, a sweatshirt, two pairs of shoes, and one dress. I guessed I'd wear the dress, which was orangey yellow like saffron, with sprigs of flowers sprinkled over the skirt, and a denim vest to match. Mae-Mama had bought it for me on sale at Wal-Mart.

Granny Zook smiled. "Oh, Lizzie," she said, chugalugging that disgusting milk, "you're not expected to attend church. The Amish don't take too kindly to sod visitors."

"Sod visitors?" I asked, thinking that sounded like somebody who might pay a call to a clump of dirt.

"English," said Granny Zook. "Worldly folks like you and your Pa. Some of the Amish call the English sod."

"So that means they think of us as dirt?" I asked, offended. There was no way some Amish person with manure caked on their shoes was going to call *me* dirt.

Granny Zook laughed. "No, Miss Lizzie," she said. "It's just a slang word. I'm not sure where it comes from."

"Oh," I said, chomping on a fat hunk of toast drizzled thick and gooey with jelly. Granny Zook's strawberry jelly was the best: sweet and seedy and gummy with clumps of real strawberry chunks, plucked juicy and fresh from Granny Zook's strawberry patch out back.

"When is it your turn to have church?" I asked, as Granny Zook forked a hunk of that scrapple junk. This gourmet grub of Pearly Gates was pretty doggone nasty, if you asked me.

59

"Not for a while," said Granny Zook. "We each host church every few months."

"Oh," I said again, chewing. "Does Daniel Smucker come to church?"

"Of course," said Granny Zook.

I was quiet for a while, thinking. "How are you getting there?" I asked. "You don't have a horse now, since Midnight died, do you? Where's your buggy?"

Granny Zook laughed. "One question at a time, Miss Lizzie," she said. "I'm walking to church; no, I don't have a horse, but I'm getting one soon; and my buggy is being repaired down at Abe Esch's Buggy Shop."

"Oh," I said. "What kind of horse are you getting? I hope it's black like Midnight." Granny Zook had owned Midnight since I was eight, and he died back in April. I cried when we got Granny Zook's letter, telling Pa and me that Midnight had passed on and gone to Horse Heaven, where the pastures are always green and there are thousands of apple trees and it rains brown sugar instead of water. If I closed my eyes, I could picture Midnight flying.

"I'm getting a white horse this time," replied Granny Zook, mopping up the end of her breakfast with a piece of bread. "He is the son of Blizzard."

Blizzard. The most beautiful horse I'd ever seen. "Daniel Smucker's Blizzard?" I asked, and Granny Zook nodded.

"What's the white horse's name?" I asked, and Granny Zook shrugged, standing with a hiccup and clomping to the sink.

"He doesn't have one just yet," she said, swabbing her mouth with the dish towel.

"Can I give him a name when he comes?" I asked, and Granny Zook turned to smile.

"Yes, you may, Miss Lizzie," she said. "And now I need to get ready for church." I saw that the wings of her black dress were speckled with dots of ketchup, and it reminded me of those painted birds Pa told me about. Maybe that's why Granny Zook never wore makeup: it would make her too heavy to fly. This all went through my mind, seeing those ketchup dots, and then another thought struck.

What would I do while Granny was in church? There was no TV, no radio, no video games, no movies, no good magazines to read. I'd brought one book, which Jo-Lynn Walker loaned to me because she said that the title sounded like something I would say. It was written by some author I'd never heard of. I hadn't started it yet, because I had a feeling it might make me cry. And I sure didn't need anything else to make me cry, not on my first day in Pearly Gates with none of the things I was used to, like my Pa. I missed Pa desperately, so bad that it pinched my heart to think of him, and it hit me that this must have been how I felt at nine months old, except I was too young to know why. I was too dumb to know that my mama was gone from this earth forever, and that I'd just have to live my life without her.

I miss you, Mama, I whispered without words, from somewhere deep and quiet in my soul. *And I miss Pa, too. I wish you were both here in Pearly Gates, and that we would be a family again, together for all eternity.*

And then, from out of the blue, a major brainstorm came my way. I'd use my time alone to search for Mama, to try to find out more about the person who gave me life.

"Granny Zook," I said, as she headed for the stairs, "do you have any letters or anything from my mama? Something that she might have written to you?" Pa had a stack of letters that she'd written, words of love for Pa on paper of many colors, tied together with a faded red ribbon. He kept them way back in the corner of his closet, but he took them out on Valentine's Day a couple of years ago and let me read them. The letters made me cry, especially the last one Mama wrote before her death.

Granny Zook thought for a minute, scrunching up her brow. "I believe I do have some letters," she said. "They'd be up in the attic, in a box labeled RACHEL AND JAKE."

My heart lifted, making tracks for the attic before my body even had a chance to move. "You have a RACHEL AND JAKE box?" I asked. "What's in it?"

Granny Zook shrugged. "Memories," she said, skedaddling up the steps, black back fading away into the twists and turns of the staircase.

"You may open the box while I'm in church," she called. "Just be careful not to lose anything."

I wasn't going to lose anything. If I found something of my mama . . . anything . . . I was going to

62

carry it in my soul forever, just as I do Pa's stories. Granny Zook shouldn't worry, I never lose a thing.

Granny Zook's footsteps thudded upon the floor above, and I closed my eyes and pictured Mama — flying — the prettiest angel you'd ever hope to see. She wore a red-and-white Phillies baseball shirt, faded blue jeans with holes in the knees, and her clunky black workboots, which didn't weigh her down any more than a pair of wings. She was flying, and smiling, and so was I.

CHAPTER 10

Attic Magic

Granny Zook's attic was just the way attics are supposed to be: crowded and crumbly and stuffy, with the
sun beaming in through diamond-shaped panes of
glass and illuminating zillions of floating dust motes.
I'd never been up there before, and it was jam-packed
with more magical attic stuff than I ever would have
imagined, crammed wall-to-wall and filled to the rafters with the things of Pa's childhood. Pa had told me
once that Granny Zook was a pack rat, saving *everything* for a rainy day, and now I saw it with my own
eyes.

There were bolts of fabric and stacks of sewing
patterns, quilting racks and empty feed sacks, outgrown Amish clothes and a row of headless man-
nequins, pressed chest to back to chest. Counting a
dozen plastic bodies of all sizes, I decided they must
have been for Pa and the other six of Granny Zook's
kids, at different times in their lives.

A rickety wardrobe teetered in a corner, near a

pile of old games like Checkers and Dutch Blitz and Parcheesi, Uno and Yahtzee and Monopoly and Life. Some of the boxes were torn, and game pieces were spilled every which way onto the wooden floor: circles of red and black ridged checkers, faded playing cards, a miniature silver iron. I picked up the iron, then dropped it when I noticed mouse turds mixed in with the game pieces.

The ceiling was low and slanted, and there were big timber beams held together with pointy wooden pins. Hung from the beams were sleds of many sizes and different kinds: Flexible Flyers with scraped red runners, saucers of worn blue tin, old toboggans of wood, plastic yellow two-seaters. Draped from the rafters above were hundreds of skates: big and little, black and white, hockey skates and figure skates and plain old ice skates and roller skates. I never saw so many skates and sleds together in my life, not even in the sporting goods department of Wal-Mart.

Two good-smelling cedar chests overflowed with blankets and quilts, baby bonnets and big lady bonnets and hats of black flannel. I picked up a blue baby bonnet, with flaps for the ears and a frazzled pom-pom on top, then dropped it when a spider crawled lickety-split from inside. I hate spiders and snakes and things that hide and surprise you when you least expect it.

Granny Zook's attic was chock-full of boxes, packed with stuff like mason jars and tin canisters and crocks and pots of many colors. There were boxes of yellowed flaking newspapers and ancient greeting cards and feed mill calendars from years gone by. There was a box for each of Granny Zook's kids, labeled in order: MELVIN, JOHN, DAVID, ELI, ANNA, SARAH, and JAKE. There was a box for each of the fourteen grandchildren; mine was a tattered Quaker Oatmeal carton marked with a big LIZZIE ZOOK. But where was the RACHEL AND JAKE box?

I took a deep breath, smelling cedar and musty clothes and mothballs and dust. *Where's the box, Mama? Granny Zook says that she has a RACHEL AND JAKE box. Where is it?*

Sighing, I flipped through the stack of calendars, going back in years as I neared the bottom of the pile. And then I found the one I was looking for: 1984, the year I was born. Catching my breath, I yanked out the calendar, flipping through the months. On January 28, Granny Zook had written: "Rachel's baby due to arrive." Then, on February 2: "Girl baby born at 7:53 A.M. Named Elizabeth Rachel Zook."

I skimmed the calendar, scanning the months for anything else about me, or Mama, or Pa. Nothing . . . just Granny Zook's doctor appointments and quilting circle dates and visiting for singing days.

I pushed frizzy hair from my eyes, trying to find the RACHEL AND JAKE box. I looked high and low, up and down, until — from out of the blue — a black bat flapped through the attic, thwacking its wings hard against a closed diamond-shaped pane of glass. I jumped almost out of my skin, and cowered in a corner. Ever since I was nine, I've been kind of terrified of bats, after a brown furry one flew into the silver-and-green submarine one summer night when I was home alone.

66

I had to open every window in the trailer to get the thing out.

Hunkered down behind a pile of boxes in Granny Zook's attic, I thought of what I'd learned in science class about bats: they're the only mammals that fly. Their wings are thin skin stretched from front to back legs, and from back legs to the tail. Their long skinny finger bones act as wing struts, stretching the skin tight for flying. They fly on their fingertips.

The bat was flying, then it crash-landed on a beam, folding its wings alongside its ugly mouselike body and nestling down. Bats usually roost upside-down. I wondered what was wrong with this one. I waited a few minutes, then took a deep breath and stuck my neck out, gathering my courage and an empty box to trap the bat. Tiptoeing and practically holding my breath, I snuck up on the thing, hoping that bats wouldn't attack if they were scared. I remembered our science teacher, Mr. Witwer, saying that bats are really timid creatures, and that those stories you hear about bats tangling in people's hair are just old wives' tales. Mr. Witwer said that bats are actually much nicer than most folks know. I hoped that held true for this particular bat.

Skulking up behind the beam, I leaned forward and peeped at the tar-black critter. I was quivering almost as much as the bat's pointed ears. And then I saw it: a baby, an itsy-bitsy bat baby with closed eyes and pinkish skin, curled up all snuggly and nursing on its mama. I dropped the box and stumbled backwards, blundering onto the top of a cardboard box draped by a fringed black Amish shawl. As the shawl slipped off, I saw the words RACHEL AND JAKE, scrawled all squiggly and sloping on the lid of the box.

This was the next best thing to a miracle: losing my wits and finding what I was looking for, all because of a couple of bats. Seemed like attic magic.

"Thank you, Mama," I breathed, bending to lift the box into my arms. "Thank you, Mrs. Bat," I added, knocking over a naked mannequin and wasting no time to stop and pick it up.

I made a beeline for the staircase, pressing the RACHEL AND JAKE box to my chest. Thudding and scudding down the dusty wooden steps, I rushed downstairs, feeling as if I were skimming on air, winging to the second floor of Granny Zook's house. Who says that bats are the only mammals that fly?

CHAPTER 11

Almost Empty

The box was almost empty. All that was within the battered cardboard was a crinkly gold-engraved invitation to Mama and Pa's wedding, along with a couple of crumpled purple dinner napkins printed in silver. "Rachel and Jake" glistening from two joyful-looking bells, ringing out their marriage date: July 22, 1982. I sighed, trying to convince myself that *something* was better than *nothing*. But still, the box was almost empty, and that was nothing like the something wonderful I'd expected.

Slumped upon the dark braided rug in the room that used to be Pa's, I lifted out the invitation, holding it so that the shiny words caught the morning sunlight through the window.

"Rachel Anna Stoltzfus, daughter of Isaac and Rebecca Stoltzfus, and Jacob Aaron Zook, son of Lydia Zook and the late Eli Zook, wish for you to share in their joy as two lives become one, July 22, 1982, at 2:00 P.M., in the Little Hilltop Chapel, Paradise, Pennsylvania."

I stared at the shimmering words, thinking how golden and hopeful they were. *Two lives become one.* And then the two lives became three, and way too soon went back to being two. Pa and me, reduced to two with the crash of a car and the last beat of a heart. How quickly things can change.

Share in their joy. I thought of the stories Pa told about their wedding day: how Mama was so giddy that she giggled all the way through the vows. How they threw blue flower petals from the hill and into the valley, watching them float away in the breeze as the church bells chimed out happy and loud. How Pa sang "Muskrat Love" as they cut the cake, which was plain old German chocolate in layers, and not a show-off waterfall cake like Mae-Mama's. How Mama glowed so splendidly, all decked out in seed pearls and sequins and a flowing train of lace that made her look like an angel in white, her bright blue eyes glittering behind a veil of pure gossamer as she glided down the tiny aisle of the Little Hilltop Chapel.

The wedding words glinted before me, and I thought, maybe finding this crinkly old piece of paper *was* something wonderful, after all. Pa had never told me the names of Mama's parents. Now I could find them! Even if Granny Zook wouldn't help me, I'd ask all around Pearly Gates, and search out the grandparents I'd never known. They'd look me right in the eyes, even though they'd turned their backs on my mama, and they'd accept me whether they liked it or not. I never could understand the Amish custom of shunning someone who leaves the faith, even if that someone happens to be your own flesh and blood. It seems downright un-Christian if you ask me: ignoring your kin and pretending they're dead, just because they don't agree with your religion and way of life. This shunning stuff had to go, as far as I was concerned.

I ran my fingers over the engraved letters on the parchment invitation, wondering why I'd never seen this before. Surely Pa had one. Maybe he didn't want me to find Isaac and Rebecca Stoltzfus; maybe he didn't want them to meet *me*. Maybe there was some reason — other than the shunning — why I'd never known the parents of my real mama.

Putting the invitation back in the box, I gently lifted out the napkin, tracing the names, then the bells. Holding the napkin to my nose, I drew a deep breath, trying to smell something of the wedding. Nothing.

Feeling empty and missing Pa, I fit the lid back on the box and pushed it beneath the bed. I wished Granny Zook had a telephone. Just hearing Pa's raspy voice would make everything okay.

"I miss you, Pa," I whispered, sliding my suitcase from under the feather bed and unzipping it. I'd been so tired last night that I hadn't even bothered to find my nightgown or the picture of Mama that watched over me as I slept. I lifted it out now, propping the gold-framed photo on the nightstand, and then fished out the packet of writing paper and envelopes Pa had bought for me. Maybe I'd write a letter to him later, when I was more in the mood to string feelings into words and put them on paper.

I decided to do something useful, and yanked all

of my clothes from the suitcase, piling them in the bottom of the enormous wardrobe towering in the corner. Like most old homes, Granny Zook's farm-house didn't have any closets, and Pa told me it was because back when it was built, people didn't own as many clothes.

And I don't have many clothes, either. Six pairs of shorts, seven T-shirts, one dress, a sweatshirt, and a pair of jeans weren't going to be enough, not for an entire summer. I wondered how I could have been so dumb, to think that I had enough of everything to last me for such a long time.

Sprawled on a saggy bed full of the feathers of dead chickens and surrounded by walls of horsehair plaster, I stared at the almost empty wardrobe, feeling full of self-pity and loneliness and doubt. Would I *really* be able to make it through a whole summer here? Would I find what I'd been searching for all my life?

CHAPTER 12

Chow Chow, Preaching Pies,
and a Big Surprise

"Lunchtime, Miss Lizzie. Rise and shine." I was dreaming of a wedding where a bat came into the chapel, and for a minute I didn't know if the voice was real or in my dream. Then it hit me as the dream bat spread its wings and flew — Granny Zook was home from church.

I sat up, head wet with sweat, groggy and blurry and grouchy. Granny Zook loomed the color of the bat in the doorway, a vision in black, her lined cheeks flushed from walking. She cradled a Bible in her arms and smelled like sunshine and fresh air, mixed in with a bit of vinegar and onions.

"Hurry, Lizzie," she said. "I've made chow chow and cheese sandwiches, and brought you some preaching pies from church."

"What are preaching pies?" I mumbled, rubbing my eyes.

"You'll see," said Granny Zook, and then she

73

was gone, fringed cape swishing behind her like tail-feathers.

I got to my feet and stretched, groaning. My head was throbbing and spinning from not-enough sleep. I hoped we wouldn't be getting up at five-thirty *every* morning. I'd need a nap each day. Pa always made sure I got enough rest, and he would never have awakened me from a Sunday siesta.

Bumbling down the steps, I heard Granny Zook singing and banging pans and slamming the refrigerator door. She sure made a lot of noise, just fixing a little bit of lunch.

"I don't like chow chow," I said, hitting the bottom of the stairs as Granny Zook plopped a jar of the disgusting stuff in the middle of the table. Chow chow is a stinky vinegar-slimed mess of cold peppers and onions, celery and string beans and cucumbers, corn and lima beans and just enough sugar to make it tasty to the Amish people who like it. But I sure wasn't one of those people.

"Do you have any Spaghetti-Os or anything?" I asked, but Granny Zook ignored me. She was dishing out the chow chow, spooning gobs of it into two huge blue bowls.

"Grossmummy," I said, "I don't want any. Do you have any Spaghetti-Os? Pa and I always have that after church on Sundays."

"I have spaghetti," said Granny Zook. "But I don't have Os."

I rolled my eyes, flopping down on the bench as Granny Zook sliced cheese and slapped it between butter-globbed slices of white bread.

"So what are preaching pies, anyway?" I asked, as she presented me with one of those cheese sandwiches like it was a prize on that old game show, "Let's Make a Deal." Pa and I always watched reruns of that on Sunday afternoons.

"Preaching pies are dessert," Granny Zook said, sitting down, muttering grace, then chomping into her sandwich and slurping up the chow chow.

"Oh," I said, biting into the sandwich and sliding my bowl of chow chow towards Granny Zook's side of the table.

"You know that RACHEL AND JAKE box?" I asked. "Well, I found it, but there weren't any letters: just a wedding invitation and a couple of purple napkins."

"Hmmmmm," said Granny Zook, crinkling her brow as she chewed on chow chow. "I know I had letters, but where could they be?"

"Maybe in the attic," I said. "Oh, and guess what I saw up there?"

Granny Zook shrugged, pushed up her glasses, and went on eating.

"A bat," I announced. "A mother bat with a baby."

Granny Zook nodded. "Plenty of bats in Pearly Gates," she said. "You'll see, come summer nights when we're working outside in the dark."

Working outside in the dark? I always thought that a workday ended when the sun went down. What had I gotten myself into? I felt tired just thinking about it.

75

But then I remembered the main reason I'd come to Pearly Gates: to search for my mama. And I'd find her, if it was the last thing I did.

"Granny Zook," I said, "do you know Isaac and Rebecca Stoltzfus?"

Granny Zook didn't answer, and it was quiet — just the ticking of the clock and her spoon clinking against the bowl.

"Granny Zook," I said again, "do you know my mama's parents: Isaac and Rebecca Stoltzfus?"

Granny Zook swabbed her mouth. "No," she said. "I do not."

But I thought all the Amish knew one another, in a place like Pearly Gates.

Granny Zook jumped up and marched to the counter, lifting a plate. "Now," she said, "it's preaching pie time."

She traipsed back to the table, and handed me a half-moon-shaped crescent of dough, with crimped edges and cinnamon sprinkled on top.

"What is it?" I asked, licking the cinnamon.

"Preaching pie," Granny Zook said. "It's dried apple pie, used in church to keep the children quiet."

"*Dried* apples?" I asked, and Granny Zook nodded.

"They don't drip," she replied. "Leaves the little ones neat and clean."

I took a bite, and it was okay — kind of sweet and dry and chewy. It wasn't exactly a Ding-Dong or a Devil Dog, like I snacked on back home, but it was okay.

And then, as I gnawed on the dry preaching pie, Granny Zook announced something that almost knocked my pumpkin socks off.

"My new horse is in the barn," she said. "Daniel Smucker brought him up after church."

The new horse! The son of Blizzard. I couldn't wait to see him. Wolfing down my dessert in one gobble, I left behind our lunchtime of cheese sandwiches, chow chow, and preaching pies, making tracks for the barn.

CHAPTER 13

Head-over-Feet
and Tickled Pink

I let out a whoop as I opened the door and got an eyeful
of the most excellent horse anybody could ever hope
for. The horse was glorious: magnificent and star-
colored, so silvery-white that it took my breath away.
He stood strong and awesome and grand, even more
beautiful than Blizzard, serenely munching on hay in
a sun-spangled stall of the barn. I was tickled pink by
the spectacle of this gorgeous, supremely white crea-
ture.

And then I caught a glimpse of something else:
Daniel Smucker, hovering quietly by the side of Granny
Zook's new horse, like a plain-clothes cop or a guardian
shepherd boy or something. You would have thought
he was the official Keeper of the White Horse, the way
he kept his eyes stuck to that animal.

"Oh . . . hello," I stammered, stopping dead in
my tracks. "I thought you had just walked the horse
up and then left."

"No," he said, flashing those Kool-Aid eyes in my direction. I'd never seen eyes so green in all my days; they put me in mind of Mae-Mama's dishwashing detergent held up to bright light. "I'm staying for a while, until he gets used to his new home and people."

"Oh," I said, half wishing I'd taken a bath and washed my hair after the morning chores. Daniel Smucker looked neat and clean, all slicked up in immaculate black church clothes, and I was kind of embarrassed to have an Amish boy see sod looking so grungy.

"Daniel," I said, suddenly struck by a thought, "do you know Isaac and Rebecca Stoltzfus?"

Daniel was quiet for a while, and there was just the chomping of the white horse, some birds singing outside, and the beating of my heart, hopeful and hard. "No," he finally said, tipping back his black hat. "I do not."

My hopes fell to the straw, and I bit my lip, thinking. Daniel should know them . . . His father would surely know them. Will I ever know them . . . the grandparents I never met?

I decided to change the subject before Daniel got nosy, and asked why I wanted to know about these Stoltzfus people nobody seemed to know.

"Can I come in there, and see the horse?" I asked.

"Sure," he said.

I climbed over the fence. "Why didn't you tell me yesterday that Granny Zook was getting this horse?" I asked, and Daniel grinned.

"You were in a hurry," he said. "Did you get the gingerbread porch?"

"Yep," I said. "And a couple of lightning rods and a mantel, too." We looked at one another and smiled, that private kind of joke passing between us again, and then Daniel looked away, ears red beneath the black hat.

"Come meet your grandmother's new horse," he said.

I shuffled close, moving slow, and the white horse stared direct and open, clearly wondering who in the world I was. His eyes were kind and soft and warm, light brown with starbursts of reddish light shining through, kind of like apple cider or something. The mane was snow white, glossy and silky, with fringes of forelock falling forward over the horse's face like thick long bangs. I patted his back, and he felt velvety, satiny, and sleek like a holiday dress. Then the horse turned his head and licked my hand, and I was in love: head-over-feet and tickled pink with Granny Zook's new horse.

"When can he pull the buggy?" I asked, looking at my damp hand and thinking of how the horse's tongue felt — rough and scratchy, like slightly worn sandpaper.

"He'll need to be about two years before he's old enough to be a buggy horse," Daniel replied. "Mrs. Lydia will train him for the next year or so."

I nodded, wishing I would be here for his first buggy ride.

"What are you going to name him?" asked Daniel. "Your grandmother said that's your job."

I smiled, rubbing the horse's face. "I don't know,"

I said. "Something pure white, like snow or ivory or milk or stars."

Daniel Smucker reached forward and pushed up the horse's forelock. "He's not quite *totally* white," he said, and pointed to a dark blaze on the horse's white face.

I leaned close, peering at the tawny brown mark, and then I saw it: a heart. The white horse had a brown mark shaped like a heart, like the heart I'd seen on the tree. And then, in the space of a breath and the blink of a white horse's eye, a name reeled into my mind, swooshing through the air and out of my mouth. "Heartsong," I said. "His name is Heartsong."

The white horse bared his teeth and smiled, just like Blizzard did, and then he nodded. Just bobbed his head up and down, stomping his hoof and saying yes to the name, giving his stamp of approval.

Daniel laughed. "He likes it. Heartsong it is."

I just knew, on that Sunday afternoon in June, that Heartsong and I would be friends forever. I felt as if something wondrous had connected us one to another in the moment I gave him his name. Tickled pink and head-over-feet in love with a beautiful white horse named Heartsong, I told Daniel good-bye and ran outside beneath the blue sky.

CHAPTER 14

Time to Make the Doughnuts

It was still dark, sometime Monday morning, and I was dreaming of riding a big white horse, storming Pearly Gates and galloping straight into the Eat-Your-Heart-Out Cafe. Just as the horses' hooves hit the slick red restaurant floor, a sing-song voice vibrated from the silver roof, shimmying high and trembly from the sky and into my tired ears.

"Rise and shine, Miss Lizzie! It's a workday." It was Granny Zook of course, and the horse faded away and changed into an old Amish lady in a long white nightgown, her hair hanging down around her waist. It was quite a sight to wake up to, and I felt confused for a split second, not knowing where on earth I was or what I was doing there. And then I remembered. . . . I was in Pearly Gates, and today was my first day as an employee of The Zook Nook.

"Rise and shine!" Granny Zook warbled. "We have baking and gardening and sewing and cooking to do."

82

Baking and gardening and sewing and cooking. I was too tired for all that work.

"What time is it?" I mumbled, fumbling around for my flashlight. The golden frame of Mama's picture glinted in the moonlight, and the grandfather clock chimed five times in reply to my question.

"Five o'clock," I groaned, closing my eyes and feeling annoyed with the five chimes echoing through the room, taunting with that cheery, jeering ring of a dingdong bell. "Five o'clock is even worse than yesterday."

"Yesterday was Sunday, Miss Lizzie," Granny Zook said. "We only do what is necessary on the Lord's day of rest, like collecting the eggs and milking the cow. All other work waits until the other six days."

The other six days. Did Granny Zook mean that we'd be baking and gardening and sewing and cooking six days a week? Why, even Pa got Saturdays off and never worked past dark.

I opened my eyes, rising up and struggling to my feet. This wasn't as easy as I'd thought it would be, and the week hadn't even started yet. Sunday now seemed like a piece of cake, compared to what today was supposed to bring.

"Wear your oldest clothes, Lizzie," Granny Zook called from the bathroom. "Gardening is dirty work. We'll be scrubbing red beets and whitewashing the trees, too, after baking the day's supply of whoopie pies."

Scrubbing red beets and whitewashing trees? Baking a day's supply of whoopie pies? What did

Granny Zook think I was — some kind of slave or something? I'd work my fingers to the bone, doing all that stuff.

"How many whoopie pies do we need to make, anyway?" I mumbled, as Granny Zook reappeared miraculously dressed in the doorway. Her prayer covering shimmered white in the moonlight.

"Oh, we sell about six dozen whoopie pies a day in the summer," Granny Zook reported, casual as all-get-out.

Six dozen whoopie pies? How in the world would we have time to do all that baking? Shoot, it took me and Mae-Mama a whole day to make two dozen cookies once, what with burning a couple of batches and having to go out and buy extra sugar.

"And on Mondays, we make five shoofly pies, along with several loaves of bread and some molasses cookies."

Five shoofly pies? Several loaves of bread . . . molasses cookies? Granny Zook must have thought I was *Amish* or something, if she even believed in her dreams that I could whip up that much grub in one day.

"Oh, and I forgot to tell you, The Zook Nook sells doughnuts now, Amish *fastnachts*, deep-fried and raised."

Amish *fastnachts*. . . . "Time to make the doughnuts," I mumbled, imitating the old Dunkin' Donuts commercial Pa always acted out to make me laugh. It wasn't so funny when it was *me* having to drag myself from a nice sound sleep, just to make some doggone doughnuts for other people to eat.

"I'll be outside a while, mixing up the lime and water for whitewash," Granny Zook reported.

"Why are we whitewashing trees, anyway?" I asked, and Granny Zook pulled her glasses from a pocket, perching them on her nose.

"To keep the bugs away," Granny Zook replied. "And to make them look pretty."

Look pretty? Who in their right mind whitewashes trees? That reminded me of how people used to paint birds, trying to make them even more beautiful, and ended up killing them. I couldn't imagine making a tree any more pretty than it already was.

"Oh, and Miss Lizzie," Granny Zook said, "today is special. We'll be making laundry soap."

"Making laundry soap?" I flung open the wardrobe door, aiming my flashlight at the tiny pile of clothes. Everything was old; *all* my clothes were work-clothes.

Granny Zook nodded. "We'll make laundry soap from meat scraps and lye," she reported. "Then when it's dry, you can cut it into any shape you wish."

"Oh, hooray," I muttered, being sarcastic as Granny Zook bustled away. Homemade laundry soap? Didn't she ever hear of Tide or Yes or Surf or Arm & Hammer?

"Meat scraps and lye," I grumbled, pulling on a pair of shorts. "Oh, brother."

And then, wishing I was dreaming and could just go back to sleep, I stumbled downstairs for my first day as an employee of my Granny Zook, a slave driver who expected me to work in the garden and sew and cook, whitewash trees and scrub red beets and make laundry soap and bake like a Betty Crocker in Amish clothes . . . all in the space of one short day.

"Time to make the doughnuts," I muttered again, navigating the twisty steps and heading into the darkness of early morning, on a Pearly Gates day bound to be a struggle of drudgery and toil, trials and troubles, and task after task after task. I'd never laugh at that stupid commercial again.

CHAPTER 15

Weary to the Bone

By sundown on Monday, I had raw, aching hands that were stained dark red, whitewashed knees, and splatters of beaten yellow egg on my face. I had flour dusting my hair and sewing needle pricks on my index fingers and a hot oil burn on my right wrist. My eyes stung from the stench of lye, and my stomach churned from the sight of meat scraps, all cooked up with water and salt until the meat dissolved into one disgusting mess of liquid laundry soap. And now it was cool: hardened into a huge ugly glob of kettle-shaped lump that Granny Zook planned to wash my clothes in. *Yuck.* I'd sooner wear the same dirty clothes all summer than try to clean them in that slop.

"All right, Miss Lizzie," said Granny Zook, still peppy and brisk as the sun sunk behind the Pearly Gates horizon, "you may cut the soap into shapes."

"Shapes?" I asked. "How will I do that?"

"With a knife," Granny Zook said with a shrug, bustling off zippy and quick, flipping the CLOSED sign from the roof of the roadside stand. I watched her go, wishing that the wings of her long black dress would simply launch her off into Oz for a couple of days, just so I could get a break.

"With a knife," I mimicked, making like Granny Zook and bustling into the kitchen, pretending I had wings and a prayer covering and was the boss of somebody like me.

I yanked a knife from the drawer, wishing it was the end of the summer already. I missed Pa, I missed home, and I was so tired. So wasted and worn, weary to the bone and ready to drop, so dog-tired that I could have slept from now until next Christmas. Now I knew how Pa felt after a day in the coal mines: tuckered out and dead on his feet, fed up and ready to sleep just so he could get some relief.

I miss you, Pa. I wish I were home. Now I know why you and Mama left the Amish: it's just too much doggone work. It's so hard to live this plain and simple life, a stone's throw from Paradise.

"Time to cut the soap," I muttered, dragging myself outside and slogging through the yard. The kettle-shaped hunk of stuff waited, blobbed by the side of the gazebo.

I sighed, flopping down on one of the green wooden swings and gazing out over the Pearly Gates landscape. Fields and farms and sky and barns . . . wide-open spaces and clip-clopping horses and real flowers and beautiful sunsets. Why didn't it seem this hard from the outside looking in? How could I have thought this would be so easy?

Heartsong whinnied from the barn, and I closed my eyes, seeing a whirlwind of shoofly pies and whoopie pies and loaves of bread, Amish *fastnachts* and molasses cookies and cleaned red beets and dirty eggs and pails of milk, spinning round and round in circles of drudgery and work. I saw laundry soap and whitewashed trees, beaters whirling through chocolate and molasses and flour and sugar, cream and yeast and oil and eggs.

It was a marvel the Amish ever had time to eat, what with all the time they spent baking and cooking and gardening. I wondered if my mama had ever worked like this, back when she was a kid. If only I could find Isaac and Rebecca, maybe they would tell me. Maybe they would show me a side of Mama that Pa never knew, a Mama that was little and Amish and weary to the bone from work.

I was so glad they had left the Amish. Baked goods whirled through my mind, making me dizzy and sick. What if they had stayed, and I was Amish? What if this was my life: baking and gardening and sewing and cooking, with no hope for college or a career or anything but having kids and making whoopie pies for all my days on earth? The thought made me nauseous, and I wondered why Granny Zook seemed so happy.

"I am *unser Satt Leit:* the Amish sort of people," Granny Zook had related today, as we yanked weeds in the garden. "And the English are *anner Satt Leit:* the other sort of people."

I was sure glad to be *anner Satt Leit,* especially after this back-breaking day. I had never worked this

89

hard at home, not even after Mae-Mama came into our lives.

Nellie mooed from the meadow, and I shuddered, remembering how it had been this morning, milking a cow for the very first time.

"Squeeze and press, squeeze and pull, in rhythm like singing a song," Granny Zook had said, as I gritted my teeth and grasped Nellie's dangling pink udders. This wasn't like any song I ever sung, sitting on a rickety wooden stool and yanking milk from a bloated cow, watching it squirt into the pail in thin streams of white. I wondered how I could have ever thought that Mae-Mama nursing Lucas was so gross. Milking a cow was a zillion times worse than my stepmother feeding my baby brother.

The udders felt like rubbery tubes of gushy fat, and it gave me chills listening to the squirting sound of lukewarm milk spurting into the tin pail. Nellie had an odd smell, too, kind of like poop and sour milk and bad breath, all rolled up into one disgusting clump of black-and-white cow. She had gas from eating so much grass, and no manners at all. Cows aren't all they're cracked up to be, believe me. Sure, they look pretty on postcards and all, but if you can get past the stink and come close, they'll gross you out in about two minutes flat, chewing their cud and passing gas and plopping cow pies wherever they darn well please. And guess what cuds are? Barfed-up food, brought back from the first stomach to be chewed again and again. *Yuck.* The thought made me queasy, and I opened my eyes, trying not to think about cows as I took a break on the gazebo swing.

I didn't want to think about cows or chickens or sheep, milk or eggs or pies, gardening or baking or sewing or cooking. I'd had enough of all that, and all I wanted now was rest. Rest and sleep and relaxation and dreams, relief from the daily grind that was Monday. I sighed, dragging myself up from the swing and picking up the knife, ready to cut shapes from homemade laundry soap.

I wondered what shape I should make as I sliced into the cooled mess of meat scraps and lye — not quite sure what form the soap would take. But then, as I cut and cut and cut, a large crooked heart began to take shape from the kettle-shaped lump of goop that we'd cooked.

I was weary to the bone and too tired to hope for anything more than the miracle of stretching out on a bed full of the feathers of dead chickens, closing my eyes and escaping from the drudgery and the toil, the trials and the troubles, and the tasks after tasks after tasks.

And then, as I lifted up my heart of soap and plodded toward the porch, I heard the sharp jangle of a ring, piercing high and loud through the evening air. It was a telephone, ringing again and again, jingling insistently from the direction of Granny Zook's barn.

CHAPTER 16

Phone Booth in the Sky

I looked around for Granny Zook. She was nowhere to be found. The thing just kept on ringing and jangling from somewhere near the star-shaped window of the barn.

Dropping my soap heart, I made a beeline for the barn, bursting through the door and running past Heartsong, going like lightning up the steps that led to the loft.

And then I saw it: a ramshackle wooden booth, shabby and broken down, with an old-fashioned black wall telephone hung inside. *A telephone!* I dashed into the booth and snatched up the receiver, breathing hard and fast.

"Hello," I panted, still not quite believing my eyes and ears. Maybe I'd fallen asleep and this was a dream.

"Lizzie!" It was Pa, and his familiar voice coming from such a strange place hit me like a ton of bricks, in this rickety and unexpected phone booth in the sky.

I took a deep breath. "Pa," I said, "I didn't know Granny Zook had a telephone in the loft. Why didn't you tell me?"

Pa sighed. "Grossmummy never wanted folks to know," he said. "It's been there since I was a kid."

"But . . . but," I stammered, all rattled and in a fog of weariness and shock, "the Amish don't believe in telephones."

"The Amish *Church* doesn't believe in telephones," Pa said. "But some of the Amish like the convenience, so they hide phones in basements or barns."

Unglued and without a clue, I lashed out at Pa. "But that's like lying!" I cried. "Or cheating! And I thought that the Amish were so perfect."

"They're of this earth, Lizzie," said Pa, his words crackling through the receiver. "Nobody's perfect."

"But doesn't Granny Zook worry about her salvation, what with having something that's not allowed?"

Pa paused for a moment, and I imagined him scratching his head, rousing up the cowlicks. "Grossmummy knows that having a telephone won't keep her out of heaven," he said. "The Lord doesn't care if the Amish are modern or not, just the Old Order Church."

I thought about that for a minute, still boggled by the idea of my Amish grandmother having a hidden telephone.

"So why'd you call, Pa?" I asked, and he laughed.

"To talk to you," he said. "I figured it was worth

having Granny Zook mad at me, just to hear your voice."

"Oh," I said, smiling and picking at the whitewash on my knees.

"Guess what I did today, Pa? I got up at five o'clock, collected eggs, milked the cow, pulled weeds in the garden, scrubbed red beets, whitewashed trees, helped Granny Zook sew some of her quilting pieces, baked whoopie pies and shoofly pies and molasses cookies and bread. Oh, and deep fried *fastnachts*, too, and helped make disgusting homemade laundry soap from meat scraps and lye."

Pa chuckled. "I told you the Amish don't waste, Lizzie," he said. "Sounds like Grossmummy kept you pretty busy."

"*Too* busy," I sighed. "I'm tired." I looked at the red stains on my hands and beneath my fingernails.

"Ready to come home?" Pa asked, gentle and quiet.

I thought for a while, and then Heartsong neighed in the barn below.

"Not yet," I said. "Granny Zook got a new horse — the most gorgeous white horse you'd ever hope to see. And guess what? He's the son of that horse Blizzard we met on Saturday, with the Amish kid Daniel Smucker. I named him Heartsong, on account of the miracles in the Eat-Your-Heart-Out, and the heart carved in the tree where our little pink house used to be. Oh, and the horse has a brown spot shaped like a heart, too — that's part of the reason for his name." I was blabbering, I knew, but I couldn't help it. Pa and I told each other everything.

"And guess what else, Pa? I found your wedding invitation in the attic, along with some purple napkins. Why didn't you ever show me the invitation before? Don't you have one?"

"Oh . . . somewhere," Pa replied, vague and changing the subject. "So, how are you doing with no TV, no hairdryer, no air conditioning, no electric lights, no Jo-Lynn Walker, no radio, no movie theater, no video games, no CDs, no me?"

"Well," I said, blowing a frizz of hair from my eyes, "the air conditioning and hairdryer would be nice. But I'm too busy for all the other stuff, anyway."

"Even *me?*" Pa asked, a wink in his voice.

I laughed. "No, not you," I said. "But everything else."

"So, have you eaten any scrapple?" Pa's voice was ornery, trying not to smile.

"No way," I said, scrunching up my face. "I had toast and root beer for breakfast yesterday and today. And guess what, Pa? Granny Zook never heard of Cocoa Puffs or Froot Loops or Spaghetti-Os. And she said I didn't have to go to church with her yesterday, so I stayed here and looked through the attic."

"The Old Order Amish Church doesn't take too kindly to worldly visitors," Pa said, and I shook my head.

"That's exactly what Grossmummy told me, except she called it sod visitors. She said that's a slang word for English people."

"I know," said Pa. "I used to say it myself."

"Oh, and guess what I saw in the attic, Pa?"

"Probably every sled and pair of skates I ever had," Pa replied. "Along with all my old outgrown Amish clothes and stacks of school papers and games and baby blankets."

"Yeah," I said. "All that. But I also saw a mother bat with a baby. Oh, and I ate some preaching pies that Granny Zook brought back from church."

"Did you like them?" asked Pa.

"They were okay," I said with a shrug. "Could you send a box of Ding Dongs?"

Pa chuckled. "The Ding Dongs are on their way to Pearly Gates," he said. "I'll send you some Devil Dogs, too."

"Grossmummy eats lots of chow chow," I said, shuddering. "And she sings hymns early in the morning."

"Now you see where I got that habit," Pa said. I could hear Lucas wailing in the background, then the sound of Mae-Mama's voice.

"Mae says hi," Pa reported, and I rolled my eyes.

"Tell her I said hi," I replied. "And Lucas. Did she like the real flower?"

Pa laughed. "She loved it," he said. "But she liked the gingerbread porch even better."

I was quiet, thinking of Mae-Mama liking the porch that was once my mama's. Mae-Mama had lots of things that used to belong to my real mama: pots and pans, odds and ends, silverware, Pa, me.

Lucas's crying faded away, and Pa cleared his throat. "Lizzie," he said, "I have something to tell you."

"You do?" I said, puzzled.

"Yes," said Pa, sad and low. "You know on the way to Pearly Gates how you told me you wanted to see all the stuff of my stories: the Eat-Your-Heart-Out Cafe, the little pink house, the chapel where Mama and I were married?"

I nodded, and somehow Pa knew, because he went on talking.

"Well, Lizzie, when I finally decided to take you to see the little pink house, and it was gone, that's when I started thinking that maybe I haven't been totally honest with you."

Pa hasn't been totally honest? Pa was the most upright person I knew, trustworthy and true blue. *Please, Pa, please don't tell me that you've lied.*

"I haven't exactly lied," Pa said, reading my thoughts, "but I haven't told you the whole story of why we never went to see the chapel during our visits to Granny Zook's."

"Wh . . . why?" I stammered. Was the chapel gone, too?

"Well, Lizzie, because the chapel where we were married is also the chapel where Mama's funeral was held."

I couldn't think what to say, so I just nodded.

"When I told you that there wasn't time to see the chapel, the real truth was that I didn't have the guts to see it . . . just like the little pink house and Mama's grave and the place of her accident. Those places fill me with pain and memories, Lizzie, but I guess being chicken isn't always the best way to heal

97

the hurt." Pa took a deep breath and I could feel how hard this was for him.

"I felt guilty all the way home on Saturday," Pa continued. "I was regretting all those times I could've taken you to see the pink house, but didn't."

I picked at the rotting wood of the phone booth. "That's okay," I said, shaky. Even though Pa and I were miles and miles apart, we were still so close that I could see his tears just from hearing his voice.

"Well, I've decided to make another trip to Pearly Gates in three weeks," Pa said. "Reason number one: I miss you and want to see you. Reason number two: it'll give you a chance to come home, if you want. Reason number three: I'd like for you and me to go see the chapel and Mama's grave and the place of her accident . . . together."

"Okay," I whispered, sinking to my knees and wrapping the black coiled telephone cord around and around my fingers. I was tied up in knots: loops of confusion all tangled with the shock of Granny Zook's phone booth in the sky, Pa's words, and the uncertainty of what would come in three weeks.

CHAPTER 17

Chomping at the Bit

The next five days were an endless blur of baking and weeding and sewing and cooking, working in The Zook Nook and working in the barn, working in the garden and working in the house, and by the time Saturday evening finally rolled around, I couldn't believe I'd only been there for one week. It felt more like a year.

It was sundown and I was cleaning up the roadside stand, stashing away pies and cookies and produce and bread, folding quilts to lug inside, and scrubbing down the counter. The Zook Nook was closed on Sundays, and was I ever glad. It had gotten to the point where I was even *dreaming* of selling pies to customers, answering stupid questions about Pearly Gates, and telling tourists that No, I wasn't Amish. Those sod visitors sure were something, thinking that everybody behind a roadside stand must be Amish, no matter if that person was wearing shorts and had loose flowing hair. Boy, tourists sure are dumb. I could have told them I was Amish and charged them ten dollars to

take my picture, and they would have fallen for it —
hook, line, and sinker.

I looked around as I flipped over the CLOSED
sign, seeing everything in a different light than I had
last week. Where before I had seen only beauty, I now
saw work — work in the white stucco farmhouse, work
in the barn, work in the chicken house. Shoot, there
was even work in the *flowers:* weeding and watering
and mulching and fertilizing. Now I knew why Mae-
Mama stuck with *fake* flowers.

Daniel Smucker was working for Granny Zook
today, tending the crops. I could see him from here:
blonde and tall and strong, his black hat silhouetted
against the twilight background of setting sun and sky.

A bat flapped through the dusk, fluttering wings
etched dark upon the evening streaks of purple and
pink and red and orange. I didn't even flinch; I'd seen
lots of bats in the past week.

Heartsong was in the meadow, gazing at me with
those apple-cider eyes, and I scooped a handful of sugar
from one of the sacks on a shelf of The Zook Nook.
Heartsong loved sugar.

"I have your treat, Heartsong," I called, making
tracks to the fence in filthy bare feet. My favorite
pumpkin socks were missing from the washline this
morning, and Granny Zook figured they must have
blown off in the June breeze, maybe ending up at her
neighbor Elsie's. I wasn't too worried about getting
them back; they'd been washed in meat scraps and lye.
Shoot, they could fly clear to *Oz*, for all I cared. Homemade laundry soap just isn't my cup of tea, I guess.

"Here you go, Heartsong," I said, holding my hand palm up over the glossy white picket fence. I'd *painted* that entire fence, on Wednesday, after I brushed and fed and exercised Heartsong. There was a lot more work in horses and white picket fences than I ever would have guessed, too.

Heartsong snuffled the sugar, licking every last grainy bit with his sandpaper tongue, and then graced me with one of those funny smiles, equine-style. I laughed and stroked his velvety nose, then planted a smooch smack dab on his face. Now that I'd known him for almost a week, I was even more head-over-feet and tickled pink with Granny Zook's new horse, even though he *was* a heck of a lot of work. I guess horses are kind of like babies: you love them to pieces, but they sure do keep you busy.

I wondered if my mama ever loved a horse this much. I gazed into the starbursts of Heartsong's eyes as if I might find an answer there. I remembered Pa telling me that when he first met Mama, and she was still Amish, she'd owned one of the fastest black trotters in Pearly Gates. I bet Mama loved that horse, and took good care of him, just like she took good care of me. I wondered what ever happened to that fast black trotter, and decided to ask Granny Zook.

Heartsong looked like the June picture on a horse calendar: dazzling white against the falling dusk of a Pearly Gates day. I wished I could paint — I would put Heartsong on paper and save him forever.

Taking a deep breath, I smelled horse and manure and something cooking in the kitchen, flowers and

101

mowed grass and meadow tea leaves of minty green, along with an odd odor that smelled like smoke. It *was* smoke — cigarette smoke — and I followed my nose across the yard, sniffing like a bloodhound on the trail of something. The air was reeking of it now, and the smell seemed to be coming from somewhere out back, in the direction of the field where Daniel worked. I coughed, going toward the smoke and the cornstalks, and then guess what I saw? Daniel Smucker, *smoking*, blowing stinky clouds into the clean Pearly Gates air as he hunkered between string-bean plants and cornstalks tall and green.

"Hey," I said, sneaking up behind him. Daniel jumped, scared out of his skin, I guess, then stubbed out the cigarette.

"I can't believe you *smoke*," I said, shaking my head. "Maybe you think you're sowing your stupid wild oats or something, but I'll tell you one thing: it's sick. Your lungs are probably black as tar."

Daniel Smucker shrugged, and I rolled my eyes.

"How can you *smoke* when you're Amish?" I asked. "You're supposed to be so doggone perfect."

"My pop grows tobacco," Daniel said, green eyes aimed straight at mine. "Tobacco is for smoking."

I crossed my arms, blowing a frizz of hair from my face. "Well, how does your dad explain doing something that *kills* people?" I asked, and he shrugged again.

"We're not perfect," he said. "No more than you are."

"You might not be perfect," I shot back. "But you

still should be smart enough not to do something so dumb." I was fuming.

"You know what?" I said. "All my life, I've been thinking that Pearly Gates is perfect . . . that the Amish are perfect . . . that my Granny Zook is perfect. The grass always seemed greener here, the sky bluer. Shoot, even the sunshine seemed brighter!"

I took a deep breath, digging my toes into the warm earth. "I came here because my mother died in Pearly Gates," I said. "I wanted to find out more about her, to see all the stuff my Pa was always talking about. But what do I find? The little pink house has been torn down, and nobody seems to know my mama's parents."

Daniel was picking at a fingernail. "Is that Isaac and Rebecca Stoltzfus?"

I caught my breath and held it, nodding.

An eternity seemed to pass, as Daniel bit his nail and looked at the ground. "I know them," he said. "They were excommunicated from the Amish."

My heart rose into my throat. "Why?" I asked. *Excommunicated.* Kicked out, given the boot, forbidden to be Amish or to associate with the Amish. Excommunication, like shunning, was one of those things I just didn't understand. Who did the Amish think they were — *God?* I couldn't figure out what gave them the right to pass judgment on others and decide who was good and who was bad, who could be Amish and who couldn't. There were no ifs, ands, or buts as far as excommunication was concerned: the Amish call all the shots, and you walk the line, or you're out . . . cut off and sent into the world.

"I don't know why it happened," Daniel replied. "But I did hear that they moved far away, to somewhere upstate in Potter County."

The grandparents I never met are no longer Amish. I was flabbergasted, feeling cheated and deceived, like all of Pearly Gates had pulled a fast one on me or something.

"Why didn't you tell me, when I asked you about them last Sunday?" I demanded, and Daniel bit his lip.

"We're supposed to no longer know those who are excommunicated," he said. "It's like a death."

"It's *worse* than a death," I said. "I still know my mama, even though she died. And I wish I knew her better."

Daniel stared at the ground and I couldn't see his face, just the top of his hat. "If you'd told me last week that they were your grandparents, I would have let you know. But I'm not really supposed to tell English people who's excommunicated."

I exploded. "And you're also not really *supposed* to smoke! You're not *supposed* to have music and feathers and dice in your buggy! And my Granny Zook isn't really *supposed* to have a telephone hidden in her barn! But you *do* smoke, you *do* have music and feathers and dice, and my Grossmummy *does* have a telephone! Now how do you explain all that?"

Then a thought struck. "Does my Granny Zook know that Isaac and Rebecca were excommunicated?"

Daniel sighed. "Of course," he said. "All Amish know when that happens."

I took a deep breath, puffing out my cheeks and

digging my feet into the cooling earth. Then, chomping at the bit and with a chip the size of Pennsylvania on my shoulder, I stomped off to find Granny Zook.

CHAPTER 18

Skeletons in Granny Zook's Cupboard

Grossmummy had some skeletons in the cupboard, and I was going to find them if it was the last thing I did. I'd pry Granny Zook's secrets from her lips and keep a stiff upper lip, no matter *what* she told me.

"Granny Zook!" I yelled, storming into the kitchen. "I have some questions for you."

"No need to yell, Miss Lizzie," said Granny Zook, hunched over the stove and stirring something in a pot. "I'm right here."

"Why didn't you tell me that my mama's parents were excommunicated?" I blurted out, sinking onto a bench at the table.

Granny Zook pressed her lips together, then turned off the stove. She clomped over to the table and sat across from me.

"We're not supposed to tell," she said. "And Isaac and Rebecca didn't want Jake to know."

"They . . . they didn't want Pa to know?" I stammered. But Pa was their son-in-law, even though they did shun him. Why wouldn't they want Pa . . . and me . . . to know? We would be able to get together now that they didn't have to shun us anymore.

"They didn't want your father to know about their excommunication," Granny Zook said, "because they are ashamed. It's a terrible thing to be excommunicated, and so shameful when one has *tried* to live the right kind of life, but failed. Isaac and Rebecca didn't want you and your father to know, because of the shunning."

"The shunning?" I asked, and Granny Zook nodded.

"They were supposed to shun you and your pa," she said. "And they tried their best, but it hurt them. That's why Rebecca served as the midwife when you were born."

The midwife? The Amish lady who helped bring me into this world in the little pink house? Pa had never told me that Mama's mother was the midwife.

"You didn't know yet that Rebecca was the midwife," Granny Zook said, more a statement than a question. "Your pa was waiting for the right time to tell you."

Pa had secrets, too? All these skeletons tumbling from Granny Zook's cupboard were shocking to me. I didn't know if I could stand any more from Pa.

Granny Zook reached across the table and took my hand, holding it tight in hers. "Rebecca and Isaac loved your mama with all their hearts," she said. "And their hearts were broken when she left the Amish, just

107

as mine was broken with your pa. But even though their hopes and hearts were broken, they still loved their daughter. The Church required that they shun your mama and pa, but Isaac and Rebecca couldn't bear to completely shut them from their lives. So they did some sneaky things: like having Rebecca work as the midwife, so that she could see you and your parents."

"Did the Church find out?" I asked, my voice breaking, and Granny Zook nodded.

"Somehow, they found out," she said. "And Rebecca was warned not to break the shunning again."

"Was she excommunicated because of helping with my birth?" I asked, trembling.

"Not only that," said Granny Zook with a sigh. "Lots of things. The Church discovered that Isaac and Rebecca were hiding a camera, a television, and a telephone in their home. Those were the straws that finally broke the camel's back. They were excommunicated."

I took a deep breath. "But *you* have a telephone," I said. "Pa called me on Monday, and told me you've had it since he was a kid."

Granny Zook dropped her eyes. "I do have a telephone, Lizzie," she said. "I'm not supposed to, but I feel more prepared for emergencies. At my age, one never knows what will happen. But if the Church found out, I could be excommunicated."

"So why don't you just leave the Amish, like Mama and Pa did?" I asked. "Then you could have a telephone and it would be nobody's business."

Granny Zook sighed. "Being Amish is my life, Lizzie. It's all I've known for sixty-nine years, and I'm too old to change now. Not only that, I like being Amish. I like the sense of community, the close-knit people, the peace and comfort in my soul of knowing who I am and where I'm going someday. I like being not of this world, and not part of the rat race ways of the English. I am *unser Satt Leit*, Miss Lizzie, and always will be. It would kill me to be released from the Amish and sent out into the world."

Granny Zook looked at me, and there were tears shimmering in her faded blue eyes. "It's not easy being Amish, Lizzie," she said. "We strive for perfection, yet we are still human. This creates a struggle within the soul that sometimes causes a breaking away, such as with your mama and pa. Some people just long for the things of the world, and tire of trying to live a perfect life."

"But *nobody's* perfect," I said, and Granny Zook nodded.

"That's right," she said. "And that's why I have a telephone in the barn. That's why Daniel Smucker smokes, and has a radio hidden in the buggy. And that's why I haven't shunned you and your pa."

My heart caught in my throat. "You're *supposed* to shun us?" I asked, and Granny Zook nodded sad and slow.

"Yes, I am," she said. "It was ordered when your mama and pa left the Church that I was to shun them and their family. But I couldn't, Miss Lizzie . . . I just couldn't. I love you all too much." Granny Zook was crying now, tears trickling down her crinkly cheeks.

"If the Church found out, you'd be excommunicated," I said, seeing the light as to why I didn't go to church with Granny Zook.

"I might be excommunicated," Granny Zook said, wiping her tears and trying to smile. "But if I was sent out because of loving you, I have to think that it would be worth it."

My eyes filled and my heart swelled, so full of love for Grossmummy at that moment that I could have hugged her till eternity.

"But Daniel Smucker knows that I'm not shunned," I said. "And any other Amish who see me working here."

"Daniel Smucker keeps my secrets and I keep his," Granny Zook said with a wink. "And the other Amish assume you're just a sod visitor I hired for the summer."

I started to laugh. "So how many more secrets are you keeping, Grossmummy?" I asked, only half kidding.

"Oh, just a few," she replied. "Like the fact that my black horse Midnight used to be your mama's horse when she was Amish."

"Midnight," I gasped. "That was Mama's fast black trotter?"

Granny Zook nodded. "Why didn't you or Pa ever tell me?" I asked, and she smiled.

"Your pa didn't recognize the horse," she said. "I didn't get Midnight until you were eight, you know, so he hadn't seen the horse for years. The horse had aged and had a new name, and your father never guessed.

110

I didn't want to bring back bad memories, so I just never mentioned it."

I closed my eyes, picturing Midnight, then Mama, then the two of them together.

"And one last secret," Granny Zook said as I opened my eyes, "is that there are many photographs of you and your mama stored in the LIZZIE ZOOK box in my attic. They were taken with Isaac and Rebecca's forbidden camera, during forbidden visits to your little pink house, and given to me by Rebecca, who got double prints of the pictures. I was planning to show them to you someday soon, when I felt you were ready to hear the truth about your mama's parents."

"I guess I was ready," I said, head spinning from all Granny Zook's revelations. "Or I wouldn't have asked you to tell me your secrets."

CHAPTER 19

More Wonderment

Up in the attic, back in a far corner, I found pictures of Mama, pictures of me, pictures of Pa, and pictures of all three of us, together as a family. There were some taken inside, some taken outside, some of the little pink house and of the yard. There was one picture of me with Rebecca, and one of Isaac and me. There were seventy-two photographs in all, along with a letter from Mama to Granny Zook, dated February 19, 1984.

Dear Mum,
Thank you for the lovely baby quilt you made
for Elizabeth . . . I will treasure it forever. Even
though we're just down the road, I wanted to
put my gratitude into words on paper. I thank
you for all the love you've continued to show
to Jake and me, along with the welcome and
love you've given our baby. I know that Eliza-
beth will be very close to you as she grows up,
and that she will appreciate her Grossmummy

Zook as Jake and I do. We realize the risk you are taking by not shunning us as the church requests. It means so very much to us that you are willing to risk the fellowship of the Amish community for the short visits we enjoy together. And Mum, I just wanted you to know how sure I am in my heart that your decision to not shun us will not affect your salvation in any way. Jake and I believe that God's love and forgiveness do not depend upon rules and tradition, and His is an unconditional love. I'll see you in heaven someday! We love you very much.

Rachel and Jake and Baby Lizzie

P.S. Thanks again for the quilt!

The tiny quilt was tucked beneath the pictures: pink and blue and green and maroon, swirls of color and shapes in a zigzag pattern. It was beautiful, and I held it to my heart as I ran downstairs.

"Granny Zook!" I shouted. "Why didn't you ever show me this quilt before?"

Granny Zook was in the kitchen, stirring the pot again, and she shrugged. "I forgot all about it," she said. "Jake left it here when you moved away, so that I could give it to you someday. I guess today is the day."

"Thank you, Grossmummy," I said and dashed back to the attic. The bat mother was on her beam with her baby, who'd grown in the past week. Pretty soon it'll fly away, I thought, picking up the box of pictures. Or maybe the mama will fly away first, just like mine. But it doesn't really matter, because they'll be together again someday.

I'll see you in heaven someday. Mama's words, written loopy and neat upon pink lined paper, ran again and again through my mind as I carried the box downstairs.

I'll see you in heaven someday, Mama, and I'm glad I got to see a little more of you now, on this earth in a place called Pearly Gates. I got to see more of Granny Zook, too, so I guess this trip was a success.

Just at that moment Daniel Smucker burst into Granny Zook's kitchen.

"Lizzie!" he called. "Come see. There's a pumpkin growing already — out in your grandmother's pumpkin patch."

CHAPTER 20

A Sacred Place

The next couple of weeks passed in a haze of days, and before I knew it, Pa was rattling in, his old pickup truck newly painted in a bright blue shade, the color of a Pearly Gates sky in July.

"Pa!" I yelled, running to meet him. Pa put on the brakes, shut off the truck, and hopped out to swing me around in a big hug. It had only been three weeks since we'd seen each other, but it felt like forever.

"Are you coming home with me tomorrow night?" Pa asked.

"I'd like to," I said. "But I haven't even mentioned anything to Grossmummy about your call."

"Well, let's go talk to her," said Pa.

We headed toward the meadow where Granny Zook stood brushing Heartsong's white coat, the wings of her black dress flapping back and forth. Pa gave Grossmummy a hug and patted Heartsong.

"I came to check up on Lizzie," said Pa. "We've all missed her so much that we were hoping she'd come home. Would you be okay without her for the rest of the summer?"

I took a deep breath, reminded that I *had* promised Granny Zook the whole summer.

Granny Zook nodded. "Miss Lizzie is a good worker, and I'll miss her," she said with a twinkle in her eyes. "But I do know a strong young man who could help for the rest of the summer."

"Are you sure, Grossmummy?" I asked, feeling guilty.

"I *am* sure," Granny Zook said. "And anyway, Miss Lizzie, the true purpose of your visit to Pearly Gates was not just to help at The Zook Nook."

I smiled, stroking Heartsong's mane.

"God works in mysterious ways," said Granny Zook quietly. Then Pa cleared his throat.

"I'd like to take Lizzie to the chapel where Rachel and I were married," he said to Granny Zook, who nodded solemnly.

"It's about time, Jake," she said.

As Pa and I drove off, I had that strange feeling again that Pa's old truck had sprouted wings. Except this time, I knew it wouldn't be the greatest adventure of my life, but the most holy. The chapel where Mama was married was the same place where her funeral was held. It was a blessed and sacred place, the most holy place I would ever see. I was sure I must have been there, but I remembered nothing. That was weird.

I chattered and blabbered as Pa drove and I told of the past weeks: the work, the secrets, the feeling of serendipity and of miracles taking place. I talked about

116

Heartsong and I talked about Granny Zook, I talked about the pumpkin in the patch and the pictures in the attic. I talked till I was blue in the face, mostly from nervousness, and Pa was turning white.

"About two miles to go," he said, and I took a deep breath.

"Was I there?" I asked. "At the funeral?"

Pa nodded, and I looked out the window at fields and farms and houses and barns, wide open spaces and an eternity of sky.

"Were Mama's parents there?" I asked, and he nodded again.

"You know how I told you they moved after being excommunicated? Well, do you think that maybe we could try to find them sometime? To go visit and get to know them?"

"I'd love to, Lizzie," said Pa. "But there won't be time this visit. Maybe next time we come to see Granny Zook."

I nodded. It was quiet for a while, and we passed a horse and buggy. "What was the funeral like?" I asked, and he sighed.

"Sad," he said. "You kept reaching for the casket, as if you were trying to get Mama to hold you. Then you started crying as the lid was closed, screaming to high heaven until I had to ask somebody to take you outside for a while."

I blinked, squishing back tears as we started up a hill. "It's right up there," Pa said, pointing to a tiny faraway chapel high on the tree-lined rise. I took a deep breath and held it, wondering if we'd go inside and say

117

a prayer or something. I knew how hard this must be for Pa, even worse than it was for me.

The Little Hilltop Chapel, Paradise, Pennsylvania. I thought of how the words had looked on the wedding invitation — golden and hopeful.

"Next week would've been our fifteenth anniversary," Pa said, as we drove closer to the chapel. It was painted white, with bright stained glass windows and a high steeple. There were two golden globes glinting against blue sky — some kind of weather vanes or something. I remembered Pa saying how perfect the day had been, back on July 22, 1982.

"There's where we stood to throw the blue flower petals," Pa said, pointing. "And there's where lots of pictures were taken."

I nodded, wondering what Mama had worn to have her body buried in the earth. "What did she wear?" I asked.

"A wedding gown," Pa said, and I caught my breath.

"For the *funeral?*" I asked, and Pa shook his head.

"No," he said. "She was buried in a green holiday dress I'd already bought for her for the coming Christmas. And she wore a mother's ring, with your birthstone: a clear purple amethyst."

I nodded. "And what did *I* wear?"

Pa thought for a moment. "A blue dress," he said. "You always looked good in blue, with those eyes."

I tried to smile. "We're almost there," I said, taking a big breath, trying to quiet my heart. *A sacred place, holy and divine, where angels fly by.*

And then, we saw it — a sign, perched bold and brassy beside the road.

THE LITTLE HILLTOP GIFT SHOP
AMISH SOUVENIRS OF ALL KINDS
SPECIALIZING IN HEX SIGNS

The chapel was now a gift shop. Pa and I were quiet, and I could hear the sound of our breathing. This holy place is now a tourist trap. That seems disrespectful or something. What's that word that means somebody stole a sacred thing: sacrilege? This is a sacrilege.

Then, feeling the ripping away of a sacred thing, I closed my eyes and tried not to cry, as Pa silently circled the parking lot and drove back down the hill.

CHAPTER 21

Sunshine and Shadow

By the time Granny Zook got home from church the next day, it was raining cats and dogs in Pearly Gates. The sky was iron gray, the clouds dark, and Grossmummy was dripping wet, drops of rainwater plopping from her black bonnet onto the kitchen floor.

I had packed my suitcase, and it was waiting on the table, beside the LIZZIE ZOOK box wonderfully crammed with pictures and Mama's letter and the baby quilt, along with a couple of purple napkins and the wedding invitation.

"Are you staying to eat?" asked Grossmummy, handing me and Pa a couple of soaked preaching pies.

"I don't think so, Mum," said Pa. "I'm treating Lizzie to lunch at the Eat-Your-Heart-Out Cafe."

There was a knock at the door, and it was Daniel Smucker, drenched and holding out dribbling pumpkin socks. "You may need these," he said, grinning. "I found them in the yard."

"You keep them," I said. "Something of the sod world, washed in meat scraps and lye."

"And here's something of the Amish world for you," said Daniel, taking off his black hat and plopping it upon my head. "Keep it, to remember me by."

I rolled my eyes, as a drop of rain trickled from the brim of the hat. "How could I ever forget you?" I asked, smiling.

Granny Zook bustled up the staircase, her shoes clomping overhead, as Pa shook Daniel's hand.

"I have something for you, too, Miss Lizzie," Granny Zook called, making her way downstairs with a huge quilt cradled in her arms. "I once made you a baby size, now this is a grown-up quilt, for an almost-grown-up girl."

I gasped, unfolding the quilt on the table and seeing squares of bright and dark, a beautiful pattern of contrasting colors swirling in circles.

"Thank you," I breathed, tracing a yellow square.

"The pattern is called Sunshine and Shadow," said Granny Zook, looking proud of her handiwork. "It shows how things always get light again, even after darkness. The sunshine always returns, though there may be shadows."

I gathered Granny Zook's skinny body in a tight embrace, squeezing her to pieces. "I love it, Gross-mummy," I said. "I'll treasure it forever."

"Don't wait so long for the next visit," Granny Zook said, hugging Pa. "I'm not getting any younger, you know."

Pa smiled. "It'll be soon, Mum," he said. "Lizzie

121

wants to find her other grandparents, and get to know them."

"Isaac and Rebecca," said Granny Zook with a nod. "They'll like that."

"Well," I said, feeling sad to leave her, "I guess it's time for good-bye." I'd already bid farewell to Heart-song, Nellie, the chickens, the sheep, and the bats in the attic.

"Not good-bye," said Granny Zook. "Till we meet again."

"Till we meet again," I said, tucking the quilt beneath my arm and picking up my box of treasures as Pa heaved up the blue suitcase. "See you, Daniel."

"See you, Lizzie," he said, green eyes shining.

"Stop smoking," I whispered as we passed in the doorway. "It's bad for your health."

Pa and I ran outside, running toward the blue shine of the truck in the pouring rain. "Till we meet again, Heartsong!" I shouted, looking up at the star window in the barn and thinking of Granny Zook's phone booth in the sky. Well, at least I could call her now, instead of having to write so many letters.

We tumbled into the truck, as Grossmummy opened the door and stepped out onto the porch. "Safe home!" she shouted, waving, the wings of her long black dress spreading as if they could launch her off to the Promised Land. Granny Zook still looked as if she could fly.

I waved, blowing kisses, as Pa started the truck and we were off. I waved until Granny Zook and her white stucco farmhouse faded away, till all I could see from beneath the brim of the black hat was the rain, pounding hard against the windshield.

"I'm really going to miss her," I said to Pa. "Even though she did wake me up too early in the morning."

I took a damp preaching pie from my pocket and had a bite. "Hey," I said, chewing. "These are better wet."

Pa snickered and bit into his. "They are," he said, looking at me with wide eyes. "Maybe you should try putting rainwater on scrapple," he added with a wink. I crinkled my nose.

"I'll tell you one thing," I said, polishing off the preaching pie. "I will *not* order scrapple at the Eat-Your-Heart-Out."

"How about some chow chow?" Pa asked, a smile in his voice. I punched his arm, and took off the Amish hat, gazing out at the flowers and the rain and the fields. The quilt was heavy on my legs, cozy and warm. Store-bought blankets couldn't hold a candle to Granny Zook's quilts.

"I wish this rain would stop," I said. "Although it will be good for the summer pumpkin at Granny Zook's."

And then, before the words were even out of my mouth, the rain slowed and we drove into sunshine as we headed toward the Eat-Your-Heart-Out Cafe.

CHAPTER 22

Sadie of the Fake Blue Eyes

Our waitress was again Sadie, of the fake blue eyes and perky-smiled ways. She bounced over to our table, red pen poised and eyes shimmering in the silvery light.

"What can I get ya?" she asked, all cheery-like, glossy pink lips shining above a Pearl Drops smile.

"Oh, I'll try the roasted pig's stomach," Pa said, shooting me a sideways glance. "With an order of kraut on the side."

He closed his menu and handed it to Sadie, as I wrinkled my nose. "A plain cheeseburger," I said. "Fries on the side."

"And large Cokes for both," Pa chipped in as I slid the menu to Sadie. She had long painted finger-nails — metallic blue with specks of silver.

Sadie beamed and nodded and sprung away on squeaky waitress shoes, blonde ponytail swinging.

"She dyes her hair blonde," I commented. "I saw black roots."

Pa waved his hand, looking around the silver-and-

124

red Cafe as we waited for our food. The jukebox was playing something rappy and fast.

"No 'Muskrat Love' today," Pa said with a wink.

"Or Wind Song," I added. "If it had been the waitress, we would have smelled it again this time."

Pa ignored me, watching two Amish boys at the jukebox. "That used to be me," he said, nodding his head toward the boys, who were studying the song selection with squinted eyes. "Passing long Sunday afternoons at the Eat-Your-Heart-Out, spending time and all my quarters on rock and roll."

"Don't their parents care?" I asked, and Pa grinned.

"Why do you think the hitching posts are out back?" he replied. "They try to hide from the old folks."

I smiled and we watched the Amish boys, swaying in time to a Mariah Carey tune. Sadie sashayed back, holding two Coca-Colas fizzing in frosted glasses. I couldn't wait to drink a bubbly soda again, after three weeks of non-carbonated root beer.

"Do you ever wear Wind Song perfume?" I asked, as Sadie arranged the Cokes on the table. Pa slanted his eyes my way, shaking his head and taking a sip.

"Wind Song?" repeated Sadie, looking surprised. "Sometimes. I like that kind."

"Just wondered," I replied, swigging down a delicious guzzle of Coca-Cola. "I thought I smelled it."

Sadie lifted a wrist to her nose and sniffed. "Not today," she said, flashing Pa a smile.

"I think she likes you or something," I whispered, as Sadie swished away. "She keeps looking at you."

"Most waitresses do look at their customers, Lizzie," Pa said, scratching his head.

"Maybe she just likes men with cowlicks," I said, choking back a laugh as Pa tried to smooth his hair.

Pa snickered and I put my head back on the padded booth, breathing deep of frying grease and burgers and soup and good old French fries. The air-conditioning felt wonderful, and it was so nice not to sweat. I thought I must have lost about five pounds in the past three weeks, what with all the sweat and the work.

"Mae-Mama is making snickerdoodles for you to have when we get home," Pa commented. Snicker-doodles were my favorite cookies: all cinnamon and sugar and so much butter they melted in your mouth.

"How's Lucas doing?" I asked, making conversation and steering clear of the real subject on our minds — going to Mama's grave and the place of the accident.

"Lucas is great," Pa said, his eyes lighting up. "Smiling more."

"That's good," I said, as Sadie returned with two red plates balanced on upturned palms.

"One cheeseburger," she said, presenting me with one of the best meals I'd ever seen. "And one pig's stomach with sauerkraut."

"Gross," I whispered, as Sadie stared at Pa.

"You know what?" she said, gawking as Pa picked up his fork and lit into his food. "I just keep thinking that there's something so familiar about you."

Pa looked up. "Have you ever seen the movie star Tom Cruise?" he asked with a wink. "He's my brother. Twin, as a matter of fact."

Sadie giggled, as Pa poked at that disgusting roasted stomach of a pig. "This is a mighty swine meal," he said, joking around with the waitress.

"I don't know why you look so gosh darn familiar," Sadie mused, crossing her arms and scrutinizing Pa, then me. "And *you*," she said, wagging a finger my way, "you seem like someone I know, but I can't place who. It's something about your eyes."

I shrugged, and Sadie put a silver-blue fingernail on pink lips, thinking.

"What are your names?" she asked.

"Zook," said Pa, taking a bite. "Jake and Lizzie."

Sadie's fake blue eyes opened wide and she gasped, biting on the blue nail. "*Jacob* Zook?" she asked. "A son of Lydia? You were married to Rachel?"

Pa nodded, and Sadie's jaw dropped. "Rachel was my big sister," she said, and for a split second of dumbness, I thought she was joking. You know, like when Pa said that Tom Cruise was his brother. But then, it sunk in, as Pa's jaw fell practically to the floor: this was my mama's sister. Sadie the waitress was my aunt. *That's* why her eyes were so bright blue — Sadie was a relative. The realization hit me like a ton of bricks, and before you knew it, *my* jaw had dropped to the level of the burger and fries.

"Sadie Stoltzfus," Pa whispered, and the way he said the name gave me goosebumps. "Little Sadie. You were five years old when Rachel and I got married."

"I can't believe I recognized you," Sadie said, swiveling her head back and forth from me to Pa, Pa to me. "Your daughter was a baby when you moved away."

Pa nodded and Sadie bit her lip, casting her eyes down and remembering. "I was seven years old," she said. "I cried when you came over to tell Mom and Pop good-bye, and you let me hold Lizzie and try to give her a bottle — which wasn't easy, as I recall."

I gazed in amazement at this lady who was connected to Mama's flesh and blood, just as I was. The lady who was raised in the same family, by the same parents, in the same house as my mama.

"You're not Amish," I said, and she shook her head.

"I left a few years ago," she said, "after Mom and Pop were excommunicated."

"We just heard about that," Pa said. "They moved upstate?"

Sadie nodded, shoving her hands in the pockets of her red uniform. "Potter County, about three hours from here," she said. "They're doing pretty good, considering everything."

Pa took a deep breath. "Lizzie would love to meet them," he said. "And I'd really like to get in touch. Do you think they'd want to see us?"

Sadie smiled. "They'd love to," she said. "They're always asking if I hear anything of you, or if I ever see Mrs. Lydia. Mom and Pop thought the world of you, Jake. They just weren't allowed to show it."

"I know," Pa said, soft and sad. "Shunning is a funny thing."

128

Sadie was looking at me, grinning ear to ear, and her eyes were so bright and wide that I had the passing thought that they might just burst from the sockets and explode blue all over me and Pa.

"Lizzie," Sadie said, "you are so pretty. You remind me of how Rachel used to look."

My eyes filled, and Sadie leaned down to hug Pa, then me. "Let's keep in touch," she said. "You're not leaving until I get your address and phone number."

"Don't worry," said Pa. "We won't. And you're coming to visit us in West Virginia someday."

I still couldn't believe it. It was a miracle. Another serving of serendipity in the Eat-Your-Heart-Out Cafe. I'd had more magic in the past couple of weeks than most folks get in a lifetime of hoping.

"Here," Sadie said, pulling a silver chain from her neck and holding it over the table. "This used to be Rachel's, and now it's yours."

The necklace shimmered and swung in the light, and I saw that it was a seagull, wings spread wide and shiny, flying.

"She got it when you two went to Ocean City that time," Sadie said to Pa. "I always wanted to see the ocean, and feed cheese curls to the seagulls."

I smiled, thinking of Pa's story about him and Mama tossing cheese curls up into the blue sky, as seagulls swooped from high, catching the orange curls in their beaks.

"Rachel knew that I longed for things I couldn't have, like the ocean and seagulls and shiny silver jewelry," Sadie said. "She knew that I wished *I* could just fly away to the ocean, like you two did. So right after you got married, she gave me this necklace. I kept it for all these years."

Sadie bent down and clasped the chain around my neck. I felt the shining seagull swinging next to my heart. "Thank you," I said. "I'll treasure it forever."

And then, rich with some money from Granny Zook in my pocket and a silver seagull around my neck, I picked up the check and paid for our lunch, on cloud nine and flying high on the wings of a new relative with true blue eyes, just like mine.

CHAPTER 23

Crashing Back to Earth

I hurtled back to earth as the rain crashed down, storming into Pearly Gates again as we dashed from the silver-and-red Cafe and out into the gray parking lot. The sunshine was gone.

"Hurry, Pa!" I shouted, homing in on the blue shine of his truck as thunder roared and lightning slashed through the black sky.

We barreled through the rain, flinging open the truck doors and diving inside.

"Whew!" panted Pa, his hair totally soaked and flat against his head. Shivering, I draped the Sunshine and Shadow quilt over my shoulders. Pa started the truck, making his way downhill as the rain fell harder and harder.

"God's draining his bathtub," I said, just like Pa had always said when I was little and scared of storms. "And the angels are bowling."

"The lightning means strikes," Pa said, playing the old game.

I nodded, looking through the windshield at the raging sky. It was pouring, torrents of rain and wind beating against the truck. I closed my eyes, remembering how I used to think that God was mad as a wet hen whenever it stormed. Then I'd feel just a little bit mad at *Him*, for taking my mama away and leaving me alone in the rain. It was a scary feeling, but Pa always tried his best to make it better.

"Pa," I said, opening my eyes, "do you remember how I used to run and hide in the closet during thunderstorms?"

Pa nodded, concentrating on driving.

"Well," I said, facing the rain head on as Pa drove straight into the eye of the storm, "I'm not hiding anymore."

"Neither am I, Lizzie," Pa said, taking a left at the bottom of the hill. "And that's why I'm taking you here."

Pa drove in silence for a while, then he made another left, and stopped, the rain still pounding down.

"That's the tree," he said, as thunder and lightning cracked so close and loud that I jumped. "The tree that Mama's car hit."

Pa pointed and I stared, hating the big fat tree by the side of the road. I wished that the tree had been killed, instead of my mama.

"The buggy crossed the road right about here, where we sit," Pa said. "Mama swerved and hit the tree, I figured, to avoid hurting the horse and the boy in the buggy. She always did love horses."

I crinkled my forehead. "Wait a minute, Pa," I

said. "What buggy, and horse, and boy? All I ever knew was that Mama hit a tree."

Pa sighed. "I know, Lizzie," he said. "I never told you the whole story."

The whole story?

"It was a Saturday morning," Pa said, staring out at the rain. "An Amish boy was coming home from a hoedown, which is a barn party for the young folks. The boy had been out all Friday night, and was three sheets to the wind."

"Three sheets to the wind?" I asked, and Pa nodded.

"He was drunk, Lizzie," he said. "Sloshed. So liquored up that he just sat back and let the horse take the way home. Well, when the horse came around the corner and got spooked by Mama's car, the Amish fella didn't even have the reins in his hands. He was passed out in the buggy."

Pa took a deep breath. "From what folks figured, the horse reared up right in front of Mama's car. There were some skid marks, and a dent in the side of the buggy. The Amish fella woke up at the sound of metal crashing."

I caught my breath, blinking away the image of blood-red and squished orange and broken glass.

"What happened to the Amish boy?" I asked and Pa shook his head.

"He got fined for D.U.I.," he said. "Driving under the influence."

"He didn't lose his license?" I asked. "Or go to jail?"

Pa sighed. "The Amish don't need drivers' licenses, Lizzie," he said. "And it was the boy's first offense."

So all that boy lost was a couple of dollars, but I lost my mama.

"Why didn't you ever tell me that part of the story, Pa?" I asked, and he reached out to take my hand.

"You always thought the Amish were so doggone faultless, Lizzie," he said. "You seemed to believe that the people of Pearly Gates were the most perfect folks on the face of this earth. I reckon I just didn't want to blow that image."

Then, crashing back to earth just a stone's throw from a place called Paradise, I took one last look at the tree that was still alive in this world when my mama wasn't, as Pa pulled away and we made our way through the rain, going to Mama's grave.

CHAPTER 24

Peaceful Valley

White headstones dotted the green valley below, as Pa and I stood in a light mist by the side of the road and looked down at the Peaceful Valley Cemetery.

"Where's Mama's?" I asked, and Pa pointed.

"Over there," he said, and we stumbled down the hill, sloshing through mud and puddles and grass, slick and wet from the storm. Tree branches and green leaves littered the ground, a scattering of things blown from above.

I nodded, fixing my sights upon the final resting place below, the eternal home of my mama's earthly body. I'd always been kind of spooked by graveyards, thinking of all those empty and soulless bodies buried beneath stones and slabs of marble and dirt. It seemed so strange that an entire *life* could be defined after death with a couple of words on a headstone.

It was drizzling and I suddenly felt tired — so very weary that I could have laid down in the mucky meadow and fallen fast asleep. *The Lord is my shepherd; I shall not want. He maketh me to lie down in green pastures.* The twenty-third Psalm ran through my mind, as we made our way across the valley toward Mama's grave.

He leadeth me beside the still waters. He restoreth my soul. My soul had dropped somewhere into the valley of my body, as I waited with bated breath to see my mama's resting place.

He leadeth me in the paths of righteousness for His name's sake.

"Here it is," said Pa, and we stopped before a pure white headstone engraved with the shape of an angel, along with the words

RACHEL ANNA ZOOK
BORN APRIL 8, 1960
DIED OCTOBER 24, 1984
MOTHER, DAUGHTER, SISTER, WIFE.

Mother, Daughter, Sister, Wife. I reached out and touched the stone, then pressed the silver seagull to my lips, trying to push back the tears.

Yea, though I walk through the valley of the shadow of death, I will fear no evil, for Thou art with me.

"Lizzie," said Pa, "I should have done this years ago." I nodded, staring at the stone as Pa ran his hands through damp and spiky hair. Pa and I kneeled on the wet ground before the headstone, bowing our heads for a few minutes. Then, as a bird began to sing in a tree, Pa said, "Amen."

I opened my eyes, wishing we had flowers for

Mama. But then, in the meadow, I saw them. Wild-flowers — clusters of daisies and violets, yellow cuckoo-buds and lady-smocks of silver-white. They were the flowers of Pearly Gates — the real flowers Mama had loved. Pa and I didn't need to bring flowers; Mama already had them. I took a deep breath, getting to my feet.

Surely goodness and mercy shall follow me all the days of my life.

"Good-bye, Rachel," Pa whispered, standing and trying to smile at me with eyes that were red and lined.

"Not good-bye," I said. "Till we meet again."

And I shall dwell in the house of the Lord forever. Mama would dwell there forever, and I'd see her again someday. I closed my eyes and pictured Mama, and Midnight, riding the sky — flying — in heaven together.

"Amen," I whispered, as Pa took my hand.

"Pa," I said, "I'm ready to go home."

Hand in hand, Pa and I walked through the valley, and all of a sudden it hit me that I was no longer tired. I felt light and weightless, airy and frothy and full of fluffy down, just like a cloud.

I began to run, feeling as if I had wings, scaling the hill with legs like feathers. I was leaving Peaceful Valley behind, and I was flying, taking flight into the rest of my life. I was going home.

CHAPTER 25

Flying

Stars were sparkling in the sky by the time Shady Acres came into sight. Pa drove slowly up Hairy Hog Hill, as I gazed at the moon and the stars and the lights of home. Shady Acres Estates shimmered like an oasis, each trailer glimmering with electricity and aluminum and love. Twelve safe havens, laid out the same way Mae-Mama baked snickerdoodles: three across and four down.

"Almost heaven, West Virginia," Pa belted out, singing one of his golden oldies from the 1970s. *"Country roads, take me home, to the place I belong, West Virginia, mountain mama . . . "*

"You mean *Mae-Mama*," I said, changing the words and making Pa laugh.

Pa swung the truck into the driveway, and I plopped Daniel Smucker's Amish hat on my head, getting ready to hop out with my Sunshine and Shadow quilt and the box of treasures from Granny Zook's attic. I couldn't wait to see how the big quilt looked on my tiny bed, and I planned to hang the baby quilt on the wall of The Cubbyhole, surrounded by a collage of the pictures Granny Zook had given me.

There it was. Home. The silver-and-green submarine shone like a beacon in the night, ten by fifty feet of love and aluminum siding, with a gingerbread porch where the front stoop used to be.

"It's beautiful," I breathed, as Pa reached over and tilted my chin up to see the two blue glass lightning rods, side by side and spiking high into the starry summer sky, pointing the way to heaven from the roof of our trailer.

"They look like they fit just right," I said, tipping my head back and forth from the lightning rods to the porch. "As if they belong here."

"They do," said Pa, turning off the truck. "Just like me and you."

Pa unrolled his window and we sat in silence for a minute, listening to the chirping of crickets and the Sunday night sounds of a dozen different families in Shady Acres Estates. I took a deep breath, smelling lilacs and mowed grass and a delicious whiff of snickerdoodles.

"Smells like Mae-Mama's waiting for you," Pa commented, sniffing the air as he opened the truck door and lugged out my suitcase. I heaved up the box and my quilt, pressing them next to my heart on this unusually cool July night.

We walked together across the yard, and I caught a glimpse of Mae-Mama through the kitchen window, waiting, with Lucas in her arms.

"Lizzie!" said Mae-Mama, whipping open the door and folding me in a hug as we stepped inside. "Welcome home!"

Pa planted a kiss on Mae-Mama's lips and took Lucas, holding him dangling in mid-air, hanging before my eyes with Pa's hands supporting him beneath the armpits. Lucas swung loose and satisfied, draped in a plain white T-shirt that I'd outgrown . . . and he was smiling! He looked kind of like a tiny angel, dressed all in white with flappy wings for arms, flying on Pa's hands. He had some fuzzy blonde fluffs of hair flossing his head, and his cheeks puffed out pink and round. Lucas looked like the Gerber baby on the oatmeal box — all plump and happy and fat-cheeked, actually sort of cute.

"He missed you, Lizzie," said Pa. "See him smiling?"

I lowered my box and quilt to the floor, and looked at Lucas, who was beaming at me with something shiny smack-dab in the middle of his black sea of mouth. It was a tooth — an itsy-bitsy pearl poking from his lower gum, gleaming white in the kitchen light.

"Hey, Lucas," I said, taking him and lifting him up in the air like Pa did, with my hands beneath his armpits. "You have a tooth." Lucas wiggled and squiggled, and then he cooed and giggled and gurgled as I held him against my shoulder, soft sounds of happiness and contentment flowing into my ear. I patted his back and he nuzzled my neck, then grabbed the silver chain in a pudgy fist.

"That's a necklace, Lucas," I said, gently prying the chain from his hand and swinging the seagull before his eyes. "A bird. You'll probably love birds, like I do."

Lucas reached up and knocked the Amish hat from my head, and everybody laughed, even Lucas. I looked at Mae-Mama, and she was prettier than I remembered, all glowy and splashy, with her hair flowing long and silky over smooth bare shoulders. Her dark eyes were shining and she was smiling, hiding something behind her back.

"For you," Mae-Mama said, bringing up her hand and holding out a red rose. "A real flower to welcome you home."

Laughing, I took the rose and held it to my nose.

"And I made your favorites," Mae-Mama said, sliding a tray of fresh-baked cookies from the oven. Snickerdoodles — warm and sweet and soft with butter, sprinkled with cinnamon and sugar, smelling so good that I could have eaten a dozen.

We all sat at the table, a circle of family with cookies and milk, and I planted my real red rose in the vase with the bouquet of purple fake flowers. Somehow, the purple roses didn't look so bad anymore.

Mae-Mama was holding Lucas in her lap, and he started to fuss, squirming and rooting at her chest.

"Give Lucas some milk," I said, taking a bite of cookie. "He wants to nurse."

Mae-Mama looked surprised, her eyes wide as Pa grinned across the table.

"A baby nursing doesn't gross me out anymore," I said. "I had to milk a cow in Pearly Gates."

Pa and Mae-Mama looked at one another, smil-

141

ing, as I took a slow sip of milk, fresh from the carton. "You should see where this stuff comes from," I said, and they laughed, as Mae-Mama opened her shirt and offered Lucas her breast.

Lucas nursed, slurping and swallowing, and we ate, until suddenly a squishy sound exploded from the direction of Lucas's diaper.

"I'll change him," I said, jumping up to take the baby from Mae-Mama. I laid him on the white changing pad on the floor, lifting the T-shirt and opening the tabs of his diaper.

"It's a miracle," Pa whispered. "Serendipity in the Zook family kitchen."

I smiled up at Mae-Mama and Pa, lifting Lucas by the ankles and wiping his bottom. "This is nothing," I said. "I cleaned chicken poop at Granny Zook's."

Sprinkling Lucas with baby powder and arranging a new diaper around him, I bent down and nuzzled his face, and he giggled again. I couldn't get over it: my baby brother was as good as Jo-Lynn Walker's. And so was my home, and my family.

Mae-Mama and Pa were smooching, but it didn't bother me. I kind of liked it: my parents loved one another. Not a lot of kids are lucky enough to be able to say that.

Handing Lucas to Mae-Mama, I was suddenly tired . . . so tired. It had been a long day, and I was ready for night. I picked up my quilt, as Pa lugged my suitcase down the hall and into The Cubbyhole, where the fireplace mantel from our little pink house lined the back wall.

"Oh, Pa," I said, collapsing on the bed. "I love it."

I unzipped my suitcase and took out the gold-framed photo of Mama, propping it on the mantel and flopping back down on my bed. I was too sleepy to find my nightgown. I'd sleep in my pumpkin T-shirt with a seagull around my neck.

Pa bent down and kissed me good night, as I unfolded the Sunshine and Shadow quilt and snuggled beneath it. *Things always get light again, even after darkness. The sunshine always returns.* I could hear Granny Zook's voice as I started to fall into sleep.

"Good night, everybody," I called, knowing that just about everyone I loved was close enough to hear me.

And then, in the space that was all mine, I closed my eyes and fell fast asleep, dreaming I could fly, and coming home again to the place I belonged.